Woman Redeemed

Christine Ellen Blake

Outskirts Press, Inc.
Denver, Colorado

This is a work of fiction. The events and characters described here are imaginary and are not intended to refer to specific places or living persons. The opinions expressed in this manuscript are solely the opinions of the author and do not represent the opinions or thoughts of the publisher.

Woman Redeemed

Outskirts Press, Inc.
http://www.outskirtspress.com

ISBN: 978-1-4327-1583-0

Library of Congress Control Number: 2007937554

Outskirts Press and the "OP" logo are trademarks belonging to Outskirts Press, Inc.

PRINTED IN THE UNITED STATES OF AMERICA

I want to say thank you to my husband Chad who supported and inspired me to continue my writing. Also, I want to thank Monsignor George Schroeder who spent much time editing and encouraging my work. Both of these men have taught me a lot about God's Love and Grace, Thank you!

Intro

"To die upon the sea!" Our sentence was announced to the cheering crowd of onlookers. It was the only death sentence a Jewish court could hand out as it required no executioner, no killing, just a soft push out into the vast ocean with few provisions and no hope.

"Kill them!" the chants surrounded us as if one voice from a single beast. From within the crowd came an underlining growl that reminded me of those at His execution. And now, here we stood, my brother Lazarus, my sister Martha and I, Mary, condemned to die together: alone, away from our community, our friends, our people. We would drift into the open sea and, as I've been told, either die of starvation, dehydration, or simply go insane and throw ourselves into the hungry waters.

Our crime? Our belief. Our belief in Him, Jesus of Nazareth, who once held this same port at Caesarea in captivation with his teachings. Back then, the crowds of Jews, Romans, and visitors from all over had welcomed Him and us, his followers, with open arms and open hearts. What a long time ago that now seems.

Today, that close community I traveled with is dispersed. We are sent out to far corners, separated from the safety of one another to spread the Word we were taught while He lived among us. And, because I travel with Lazarus, who's own resurrection has caused fear and growing suspicion among our people, I have also been feared and hated. The growing population of Pagans into our region has brought stories of the undead, which I guess, is what my brother would be labeled. However, the same neighbors who burned our home, ran us out of Bethany, and eventually to our present fate on the shore of Caesarea, had once celebrated Jesus' miracle of bringing Lazarus back to life. Odd, how the wind changes.

Martha grips my torn and soiled sleeve as we are shoved onto the small, leaky boat. Lazarus proudly steps in himself with no prodding needed from our guards. I brush Martha's hair back and kiss her cheek, telling her we must keep faith as our vessel slowly leaves the shore. Lazarus, a hand on each of our shoulders, begins the prayers, "Father, who lives in the heavens, Holy is your name..." We join in and pray in unison watching our home, the edge of our world, drift from sight, and my heart remembers my journey here...

Chapter 1

I remember home...

The flap of a sail broke me from my daydream as I looked out over the Sea of Galilee, or as the Romans now call it, Lake Tiberias. There I sat, as I did most afternoons, allowing my long hair loosed from its ties to be carried by the wind's will, enjoying the moments that were mine before the evening meal. Fingering painted fish and boats on the blue Roman tiles of our porch, I watched ships glide across the mirrored surface of the sea against the background of the lush Golan Heights rising from the opposite coast. This lake I have called home for most of my life. Seen from the quiet fishing village of Magdala on its western coast, it was the whole world to me; and I was contented by the lapping of her ripples hitting the shore and the calls of sailors as they neared the port. If I hung my head over the edge of the stone wall, I could imagine they were dangling from the clouds that reflected on the water. And if I closed my eyes and listened to the water and the call of the occasional seagull, I could imagine I was in the center of the sea floating freely atop the water.

Some evenings, as the shadow of the house cooled the tiles, Lazarus, my brother, would join me in silent vigil over the water. I wondered what his dreams were as he gazed; but when I asked, I was only brushed off and lost my companion. So, I stopped asking and instead enjoyed the silence of his company. However, one night I discovered his mind as I heard him arguing with father.

Lazarus had been asking father if he could apprentice as a fisherman when I happened into the room. Father abruptly refused and insisted that he was pruning a strong trade business just right for Lazarus. The discussion ended with that, but Lazarus' longing hung over him like a net. The quiet, private life of a fisherman was much more to Lazarus' liking than the pushy, aggressive business of the market, but father's word was final.

In this small fishing village of Magdala, my imagination was fed by glimpses of other places and other peoples through my father's trading and the sea that brought life to many who traveled to her shores. I was a curious girl with far too much spirit to satisfy myself among the required duties of my sex. If I were not expected to learn to bake bread and weave baskets, I probably would have loved the chores; but definitions set upon me itched like camel hair and I cast them off even as a child. My mother found this infuriating, but my father found it amusing and encouraged me in spite of mother's best efforts to rein me in.

When I refused to finish my weaving, father took me to market with him to "help him unload a shipment". When I cried over having to tend the small garden we kept, father insisted that he would "punish" me by having me refold all the materials at his stall in the market. Feigning disappointment, I would sulk after Lazarus and father down the busy street toward the center of town. Once we were out of mother's view, I'd let out a yelp of joy from being freed from the domestic duties and father would lift me to his shoulders; off we were like co-conspirators headed to a secret party just for us.

At least my mother had my sister Martha whose sole purpose on earth was to become my mother. Martha never looked out at the sea, her mind never left the realities of the duties before her. If she were done with her chores for the day, she would busy herself with my chores: a whim I was more than willing to indulge. I admired her sense of duty, but feared she'd never leave the house. I, on the other hand, was out of doors every chance I got, and the best place to go was the market.

Being with my father at market brought me right in to the center of Magdala. With the docks at the edge of the long street filled with stalls, the ships I watched from our cliff-top porch were within my reach, and I could study their treasures from the deep as they sorted the edible from the non-edible. Most of the boats were local, but occasionally, the sailors from towns around the lake would drift to Magdala in their pursuit of fish. One particular boat brought our favorite crew of fisherman, including a couple of brothers, Simon and Andrew of Capernaum. They welcomed our curiosity and Andrew fed it with shells, shiny rocks, and many other tokens from the deep. His brother Simon was the storyteller; he had a story to tell of heroics upon his boat each time he came to port. Lazarus especially enjoyed these visitors as it gave him a chance to learn more about fishing.

"How do you fish with this net?" Lazarus asked our friends during one of their visits.

"Let Simon show you that, he's the expert on our boat," Andrew slapped his brother's shoulder and welcomed Simon onto an imaginary stage.

"Well," Simon began slowly, thinking of a colorful way to explain it to children, "one must have a steady arm to fling the cast net out beyond the boat's edge. There it opens like the arms of an octopus, spreading out to capture fish of all sorts. These weights here at the edge pull together and trap the fish within. And then my strong brother, Andrew here, grabs the net with one hand, like that huge Roman god, what is his name? The one who holds up the sky?" My brother and I stood dumb, we had heard a few of the Roman stories, but neither of us knew them well enough to fill in Simon's blanks, "Well, no matter. As I was saying, Andrew grabs the net and hauls it over his head and onto the boat all by himself."

Andrew laughed at the strength that was attributed to him, "I believe his name is Atlas and I've never in my life lifted such a burden!"

"Oh, but you could my brother, you could," smiled Simon.

Whether it was a story of the storms out on the water or a lesson in fishing for his pretend apprentice, Simon's tellings were always dramatic and vivid. We were not allowed to stay at the docks too long before we had to head back into the heart of the market where father awaited, but we lingered the days we found our friends docked.

Besides absorbing the diversity of the travelers who stopped at our port and browsed my father's goods, my job was to keep the stall neat and presentable, and I took that job very seriously. I did not suffer the dirty hands of travelers on our beautiful silks, but stood guard over our goods as if they were relics of Abrams' tribe. My brother laughed at my pride in my folded piles, but having me there did free him up to learn to barter, so he was kind. From there at my post, I watched my father charm customers with a smile that robbed many a man out of his hard earned money. Lazarus tried, but hardly had his heart in it.

Upon returning home, mother would insist that my nurse bathe me even if it were the second day in a row. "To clean the filth of the docks off you. You smell as if you rolled in dead fish all day", she would sneer as she turned in disgust and left me to my nurse's charge for the rest of the evening. Little did she know that if I could have, I probably would have rolled in the nets, seeking to investigate the treasure of the sea up close.

And so went our family life. Martha filled my mother's home with song and good cheer about her chores while Lazarus and I followed my father to market. We never left our hometown except for the annual trip to the temple, until one wonderful day when father announced we had been invited to the court of Archelaus, King Herod's son at Caesarea.

It was a long, tiring journey over the hilly farmlands of Galilee to Caesarea on the Mediterranean Sea. The only stop we made was a small village called Nazareth that lay half way between my home and our destination. I remember the small village and how I wondered how anyone could choose to live in such a place. Our home was alive with the bustling market at the water's edge and the coming and going of many visitors, but Nazareth was surrounded by nothing but endless fields of grain ready for harvest. Everywhere I looked, men toiled in the earth and as they swung large iron sickles, the scent of wheat filled the air. My nose stung with the dry grassy crops and I could not consume enough drink to flush it out. The houses were simple, earth-toned, and lacked any Roman luxury, so that, squinting I could not tell the walls from the ground; rather, it all meshed together. I hated it.

Of course, father had business to do so that the trip was "not without profit" as he instructed Lazarus and me. He did not direct his business lessons to mother or Martha who wandered in the back of our caravan with the other women; however, lately I had become as much of an apprentice as my brother and so I strove to stay up front with the men. Father's business was with a group of carpenters in the town: that and masonry seemed to be the only professions other than tilling the ground that this land-locked area would allow. He met with them and arranged to purchase some window lattices on our way home to sell in the market. At the announcement that we would come back through this retched village, I slumped to a stone against a wall for some shade and pouted there until the deal was completed with a warm handshake and an embrace.

As father said his farewells, I scanned the miserable room and noticed an elder carpenter, a quiet man standing on the side of the group instructing a young boy who seemed not to notice our presence at all. The bond between the two was obvious and I assumed they were father and son. I then looked to my own brother and father, and I wondered why their bond was not so rich. Lazarus and father were so different from one another and they lacked the natural kinship of this pair.

Finally, father said it was time to go. As I dragged my body from its resting place to again begin our travels, the elderly carpenter came over to me and pressed a carved box made of olive wood into my hands. I looked up, confused, and met eyes as kind as a lamb's. I guessed he had understood my frustration at waiting for the deal to be completed and wished to comfort me a bit with his gift. I bowed slightly in thanks and he smiled, patted my shoulder, and returned to his apprentice. As we walked away, I examined my present and was astounded by the beauty of the box. It was only as long as my forearm and slightly rectangular. I traced my hands over the veins of various shades, I could not feel a single splinter, and I realized it was completely carved from a single piece of wood. To open the box I had to slide the lid down from the top; inside was another surprise. Rather than carving out the entire space for storage, its maker had carved a shape in to it. I found it funny and wondered as I traced the broad opening that narrowed into a short line toward the bottom where it broadened again.

"Looks like he carved a tree inside a tree," joked my father as he saw me exploring the odd box I held. It did indeed look like a tree, or rather a bush with its short trunk. A lone bush standing on the top of a hill, but I went along with Father's tree image.

I smiled up at my father and answered his jest, "Now, I guess I have to find a tree to put in the tree in the tree." We both laughed and I wrapped the box carefully in the folds of my dress, tying it to my sash for safekeeping. I kept the box with me for the rest of the trip and decided it was a place for only the most precious articles. I could think of nothing I owned worthy of placing in such a box and hoped one day I could fill it.

Having something to occupy my thoughts made the second half of the trip much faster and when we finally felt that first sea breeze on our faces, we all took in a long, deep breath. I looked up from my thoughts and took in a tremendous sight. A graven image stood at the city's entrance and I looked to my mother who had caught up to us for guidance. Mother grabbed both us girls and turned us away from the Roman's stone figure of an undressed man. We walked into the city with our eyes covered by mother's shawl. As soon as I recovered from the initial shock, I began to struggle against her hold as my curiosity enflamed my bravery. She held fast, but I managed to part a bit of the shawl and see out. What I saw were large stone structures, a long high bridge with no water below it. Instead, people flowed through the tunnels and freeing myself from mother's grasp, I asked my father what it was.

"It is an aqueduct", he answered as if the foreign word would mean anything to me. Noticing my confused stare as I grappled with his language, he smiled and continued, "It carries water to the other parts of the city".

Carries water! I could not believe it. It was magic. How did the water know where to go? How did the water get up there? I was full of so many questions, but there was more to see. As I looked to the people I noticed there were as many Romans as Jews in the city and I stared at their short dresses; even the women were half exposed, as their dresses had no sleeves. How poor they must be, I remarked, but father just laughed and held me close as we walked.

He took us straight to the water's edge and I saw the great sea that led to all parts of the world. The breeze at once tickled my nose with the strong scent of salt that covered the entire town and lingered over the calm, clear water of the harbor. Out ahead of us we could see the stone arms of the harbor that Herod had built as they opened just enough to embrace the hundreds of ships one by one in welcome. Below us the water was so clear I could count the seashells in the sand. Father allowed us to take off our sandals and wade in to the warm salty water. I dragged my toes through the sand and watched swirls dirty the water and settle again on top of my foot. As I stepped a bit further my foot kicked up a white round stone of some sort. I bent over to catch it as it drifted in the water and could tell right away it was not a rock. It was light and when I shook it I could hear something rattling inside. I turned it over and over and noticed a leaf on what I guessed was the top. It was not really painted there, but almost carved into it.

"What is this?" I asked my father.

"It is the shell of a coin fish, and watch when I break it in half."

"No! Don't break it!" I cried, but it was too late. He poured little white pieces into my hand just as my eyes were welling up. But before a tear could fall, I looked down into my hand and stared at five delicate white doves that had fallen out of my shell.

"You see, your treasure holds a treasure," Father laughed, though to me this joke of doubling words was getting old, so I just smirked at him. Defeated, he handed me the two halves of my coin fish shell.

At the word "treasure" I thought of my box, unwrapped it from the tie around my waist and carefully placed five little birds and two white shells into it; I had found something worth keeping.

That night we were to attend a banquet at the King's palace. He was a Jewish King of sorts; his father, Herod, had balanced evenly between his Jewish heritage, rebuilding our great temple, and the Romans, the rulers of the land, building them many temples for their gods. This dual loyalty shown in the city as the blending of the cultures made for amazing sights along the way to the inn where we were staying. I saw Jewish men praying and in discussion as they walked past graven images of Caesar without showing a sign of the shock I felt at seeing the stone figures. I could not believe how lifelike they were. I did not know it was possible to make a man from stone, but the Romans seemed to have mastered the art.

Recovering from the sights, I dressed for the banquet as mother lectured Martha and me on appropriate behavior, "Do not speak. Do not stare. Do not reach for food. Do not eat until we have eaten. ..." She continued, but my mind was already at the party wondering what I would see next. And my curiosity was not disappointed.

We sat on pillows with golden threads around a table so large I could hardly see the people across the room over the piles of food before me. Seated around us were people from all parts of the Roman Empire. I saw men so light of skin that when they raised their frothy drinks in toast, I could see a light blue line all the way down their arm under only a thin layer of skin: mother said they were from the far northern regions above Rome: a large Island further than I could imagine. I saw men so dark of skin that it reminded me of the beautiful mahogany wood my father brought from far off markets; mother said they were from the land across the sea to the south of us.

With all the crowds around the tables I missed the singers who opened the dinner, but I did manage to see the dancers who seemed to have no bones, for they moved freely in ways I could not get my body to bend. I admit, Martha and I tried when my parents weren't looking, but I only managed to fall back onto the floor and knock over my dinner wine.

After dinner I climbed onto my father's lap as he spoke business with the men from all the regions and our host brought in more entertainment. I could have stayed there forever, for before us paraded animals I had never even heard of before. Small hairy creatures with hands like humans who prattled on to one another at the end of long leashes, large slow moving cats with stripes, and dogs who seemed to laugh rather than howl. I had seen more this night than I had ever before in my life. I must have fallen asleep against my father's shoulder, for I do not remember returning to the inn, only my dreams of the animals and the dancers and the fine foods of the night before.

We stayed a few more days and then began the long journey home. On the way home, I again tried to stay up with my father, for I now attached him and his business to the fantastic images of the port city, and thus my fondness for him grew.

"Why can I not apprentice at the market?" I inquired as we walked back through Galilee where men, now done with their sickles, wielded winnowing forks high into the air tossing the grain in the wind.

"Oh, Mary, you are a woman and will soon outgrow any interest in men's silly business. You will have to return to the hearth, for you must learn the business of the home. One day you will marry and your mother chides me that I have not yet allowed her to prepare you." He smiled down at me, but I knew he was as disappointed in my destiny as I was.

We returned home and continued as we had, me sneaking to the market to avoid chores and Lazarus dreaming of sailing upon the sea. I believed life could continue on like this forever, but I was growing older and my days of following father were about to be ended by a business deal made during our next trip. It was the time of Passover and we were headed to Jerusalem.

Chapter 2

I remember the first time I met Him...

Passover was the time of year when all the Jews gathered in Jerusalem. We all came: from Judea, from Galilee, from Samaria, from The Decapolis, from all corners of the region. It was a glorious sight, like floodwaters rushing back to the City of God. For days we poured in, prayed, and worshiped. But as children we found time to gather and explore the huge city. The market place that dwarfed our own is what I found most intriguing: the clinking of coins, the laughing of money changers, the women marveling at shimmering cloth and fragrant spices from far off places, the men bargaining over prices, all in the stone-tiled Court of the

Gentiles around the great temple built by Herod.

Here the Romans joined the market and brought their goods from every province of Caesar's rule, knowing that festival time was a time for Jews to do business as well as to worship. Sitting in the shadows of the colonnades that surrounded the Temple Market, I watched the sea of people while my mother joined the other women in selecting fine cloth and fresh spices to bring back home. They played like dolphins among the market stalls, chattering to one another and diving in and out of waves of fine silk and dyed wool.

Many mornings I would find a kind, young woman whom I now know as Mary, the mother of Jesus, sitting in the shade near where the Rabbis taught. She was a petite woman who seemed still childlike in her softness and in her joy that reached out and tickled your face into a smile the moment you saw her. She had a habit of gathering the smaller children around her and telling stories during the week of Passover. Women have always been the storytellers in families, but my mother did not have the flare for it that Mary did. And so, I sought her out and clung to her every word. The stories of the Exodus we heard at our Seder Meal and we had memorized the proper responses, but in the open court of the temple they were given new life in Mary's telling. She had seen Egypt, had lived there during the horrible end of Herod's reign, and she painted her memories of the sights with her colorful words:

"Our people were enslaved in the great land of Egypt, and yet we did marvelous work. Around the markets are great walls and strong stone buildings with endless steps to high quarters of powerful Egyptian rulers: all built by the hands of the Israelites. I touched the masonry of Moses' people; I walked the way of the chosen ones and heard their stories told in the paintings that mark each passageway..."

As she unraveled her yarn, I looked out at our own market. The regal Roman soldiers became Egyptian guards – their white togas grew to long gowns of earlier times. I imagined elaborate blue headdresses, black painted eyes, and stern impatient jaws. Just as the Roman soldiers paraded through the bustling Jews of Jerusalem, I saw in my mind the Egyptian guards lording over the Israelites. The clank of the ancient masons echoed in the clinking of Caesar's gold, and the same taste of dust and heat rose in our throats amid the crowds as had chocked the Israelites under their oppression. I was drawn into the history of our people as Mary continued her storytelling:

"Our people toiled under Pharaoh and the Lord came to Moses and said, 'Now you shall see what I will do to Pharaoh: Indeed, by a mighty hand he will let them go; by a mighty hand he will drive them out of his land' And Moses was afraid because he did not think he was capable of the great work the Lord had put in front of him. You see, my children, we fear when we believe it is we who are to do the work. However, if we just say 'yes' to the Lord, He works in us and we become his handmaids. And just as He heard the cry of His people under Pharaoh's rule, so today does He hear our cry."

She smiled her patient and wise grin and looked up to the heavens. We followed her gaze to the blinding sun above. As I returned my eyes to her I noticed her hand on her stomach, as a mother does when she remembers her child. She saw my questioning eyes and stroked my hair, untangling the snarls left from sleeping on the hard ground of the inn. Mary then took me into her lap and began to slowly comb out my hair as she looked to the other children who adoringly asked for another story. Here she and I sowed our bond, which would continue to grow all of our lives.

At the children's biding, she told another story. This time it was one of the many stories she had heard while in exile in Egypt. My favorite stories were of a great queen, Cleopatra, who, just three decades before my birth had shown what a strong woman of power could do. Mary told us, "Cleopatra was a woman of this world. She held power among men and seduced them into allowing her people to remain free of Caesar's control. Her long raven-black hair and painted eyes held both Julius Caesar and Mark Antony in her lair long enough to cause a break in the strong hold of the Roman Empire. She housed their armies and bedded their rulers: bearing Caesar's children and cradling Mark

Antony's heart.

"They say that when she walked, her hips swayed with the softness of the desert palm in the breeze, and when her eyes met a man's she put him under a spell of submission. She was a woman with passion, however, and that led to her end. Her passion was Mark Antony. They had a love that seemed to be created by their gods in Olympus – tragic and chaotic. They loved beyond the measure of human emotion. Mark Antony gave up his home, his family, his kingdom for her; and she betrayed her very people by choosing his love over obedience to the delicate relationship she had fostered with Rome.

"It seems in every culture that the weakness man has for a beautiful woman is often blamed for his downfall. Even as our own Eve offered the forbidden fruit, or Delilah coaxed the secrets out of Samson, so their Cleopatra lured and toyed with Mark Antony like one of her cats with a little mouse. Unable to leave his lover, Mark Antony broke his responsibilities in Rome and lost his power, Cleopatra's life, and his own to Octavian."

The boys in our small group called for the description of the battle, and though women often left those details out of their stories, Mary satisfied her audience and told of a great sea battle where Cleopatra's ships were encircled and trapped by the brutal Romans. "With no mercy, they turned then to their own rebels who fought with Mark Antony and killed every man, Egyptian or renegade Roman.

The battle continued on land and soon it was clear there was no hope for the tragic lovers."

We had often heard of these battles among the Romans and were reminded of family rivalries beginning with Cain and Able, Isaac and Ishmael, Joseph and his brothers, Saul and David; I could go on and on. I learned in the stories of our people and the Romans that great men fall by the hand of those closest to them far more often then by a sworn enemy.

"At the end of the battle, as Cleopatra and Mark Antony's armies fell, a messenger ran to the Queen and told her that her lover was killed. The passions of woman came out in her as she felt the loss and, they say, grabbed a asp, placed it on her breast, and ended her sorrows with death."

"Oh, Mary, was Mark Antony really dead?" asked one of the children who was as enthralled by these stories as was I.

"Not yet," Mary hung on to our suspense, "Unfortunately, Cleopatra's messenger was mistaken, and by the time Mark Antony got to her, it was too late. She died in his arms. In his sorrow he called a servant to him. Ordering his servant to hold out his sword, Mark Antony ran onto it, joining his lover in death."

We were astonished by these stories even more than our own; the Roman's arrogance of their power over life and death, battles and worldly control, surprised us. They did not see God's hand in any of it. For example, the act of suicide was a tragic sin to us, and yet, the Romans practiced it as an honorable death. Life, to them, was not a gift from their gods, but something they themselves possessed and had the right to do away with. It was here, with Mary, that I not only heard our Jewish stories, but learned of our Roman oppressors and their history as well.

While we were nestled around Mary, my brother, Lazarus, and the older boys would gather in the courtyard when free from religious obligations and play whatever sport they could. An old melon would often work as a ball in one of the sports they learned from the Romans; or the boys would run through the crowd, one playing a flute and the others following in procession; or, when the heat was too much to run in, they would settle around one of the mill game boards scratched into the paving stones. It is in this group that we find Jesus, a boy near Lazarus' age. They came together several years and played in the crowds together.

He stood out to me as the only one of my brother's friends who included me in the games and allowed me to follow along with them on their adventures when Mary grew tired of her storytelling. Lazarus often got frustrated that Martha, our sister, and I were welcomed, but his friendship with the boy from Nazareth kept his tongue. We all knew Jesus was someone we wanted to be near, but we didn't know why. I remember thinking He had a sweetness about Him that reminded me of His mother.

We girls were not the only ones Jesus stood up for. There was also a boy in the group who was partially lame, and Jesus protested on his behalf anytime the others wanted to run through the crowd. Bartholomew, a boy closer to my age than Lazarus', could play most of the games, but struggled to maneuver through the great mass of people as one of his legs was just a bit shorter than the other. Usually, Jesus won out, as He always seemed to come up with an alternative they could all play. And besides, I think the boys knew if they left Bartholomew out, they would lose the company of the favorite, Jesus. This uniqueness of Jesus' was confirmed for me the Passover I followed Him to the temple, or at least to the door, for I was not allowed inside without escort, even to the Woman's Court.

Every year as the sacred week came to an end, the city would empty, slowly as a trickle at first, but then as a rush of seas out the seven gates so that everyone could return to their lives. Goodbyes were said as large groups from each province left together. A caravan of men took the large bundles and started off at a strong pace, while the women, caring for the younger children, took their time in travel and met up with the men days later as they neared home. We usually stayed on, as my father waited until the prices went down to do his dealings and to gather the goods my mother had picked out during the festival week: prices fell along with the population of the celebration. Therefore, we were still there three days after the crowds one year, when I noticed our friend Jesus heading toward the temple. I was surprised because I had seen His family leave, and I had hugged His gentle mother; she and I never left without a goodbye.

Because I knew they had left, I was curious and worried that my friend was still in Jerusalem by himself. I looked around for Lazarus, who was supposed to be watching me, but he was nowhere to be seen. I decided to follow Jesus myself, but my tattletale sister Martha, of course, caught me. She was always doing the right thing, afraid of any little adventure.

"Mary, I'm telling! You are supposed to stay where mother can see you", she called from my mother's side.

"The wind took my shawl", I lied, tossing my wrap into a gust, and continuing to cross the courtyard toward the center temple.

"Yes, yes, but don't go far", my mother called half looking up from her shopping. She was much more enthralled by the silks in her hand than by our squabble.

I headed across the stone floor of the Court of Gentiles, was halted at the entrance of the temple by propriety, and hunched down by one of the large stone doors. Inside I saw the scribes and rabbis bustling about in a furry. They moved together like a hive of bees uncomfortable, restless, and defensive. I scanned the colony of men searching for my friend, when I saw him in the center of the hive. He had a scroll in his hand and was in discussion with them: the Rabbis and Scribes! I could not hear what was said, but they seemed to be reading the Torah together and as surprised at young Jesus' knowledge as we often were.

Lazarus would love to have seen this, I thought. They were both of an age to recite the Shema and Jesus had continually topped Lazarus with his knowledge of the sacred texts used in morning and evening prayer; but we had no idea He was this good. Just as I was getting up the nerve to creep in a bit closer, Mary and Joseph, Jesus' parents, rushed toward me looking frantic.

His mother cried out, "Mary, have you seen him? Jesus. We have been traveling and he is not with either group. Oh, I've lost him. What will I do?"

I wanted to calm her, but had no words; my little hand just pointed into the temple that was now audibly buzzing with discourse. I followed in behind her, unable to hold back my curiosity, and as she descended upon her son, the men parted. No one wanted to stand in the way of an angry mother, even one of Mary's diminutive size. However, as she spoke, it was not anger but sorrow that carried her words, " Child, why have you treated us like this? Look, your father and I have been searching for you with great anxiety. I believed you were traveling with the men, while your father was sure you continued with us women, and the smaller children. We were halfway home when we reconnected and discovered you were not with either group.

Why? Why have you treated us like this?"

He answered, "Why were you searching for me? Did you not know that I must be in my Father's house?" His authority was commanding and I stood staring at this bold child who held the attention of all of the adults around us. He took his mother's hand to comfort her and she at once calmed and brushed His hair with her small hand almost as tiny as His own. Joseph stood aside as if this was a matter between the two of them and walked silently behind them, his coarse carpenter hands protectively on their shoulders as they left. It was the first time I had really seen Joseph, though I had heard of Mary and Jesus talk of him. As I watched the scene before me, this older man looked familiar, but I could not place him. Then I saw his hands again, his worn, tired hands. Yes, that was it, he was the carpenter in Nazareth who had carved my precious box for me. He did not see me and I silently let them pass undisturbed.

It was to be several years before I was to see Jesus again, for part of the business fathers took care of during Passover was the betrothals of daughters, and this, my eleventh year, I was contracted to one of my father's business connections. When I returned to Magdala I found life would be very different, for mother was hurried in her preparing me by the time my womanly cycles came and we could hold the wedding.

Chapter 3

I remember the year with my mother...

Mother and I had not spent much time together during my childhood and I resented this sudden requirement to fulfill my duties. So, most of our days were quiet and she often excused herself from my training and allowed Martha to take over. Martha was much more patient, and so I welcomed my sister's coaching.

Each morning we began by going to the well to fetch water for the day. It seemed a long journey and I wished we had the aqueducts I had seen in Caesarea, but it did allow me a short visit in town before my arduous day at home. I was surprised to find that Martha had journeyed here on her own all these years. I truly had not pictured her out of the house and I was so busy avoiding chores that I had not noticed her absence each morning.

Dawn is a beautiful time to see the well. In the early morning, the road to town is cool and the splash of the sea the only sound we heard until we neared our goal. At the well there were hoards of women, talking and laughing, grasping hands and leaning in for warm welcoming hugs. As we found our way through the crowds Martha nodded greetings and shared quick embraces with several women I had never seen before. What had I been missing? I am a woman, but this whole society seemed foreign to me. I wanted to be a part of it and looked forward to fitting in. Much to my disappointment, however, when Martha introduced me to a small group at the edge of the well they smiled in recognition. Evidently, she had mentioned me in this circle. Wonderment mixed with disapproval haunted their welcomes and they stood to giggle as Martha explained to me how to raise the filled bucket without knocking against the stones and spilling it. At once I felt I was an outsider. But I was determined to fit in and studied carefully as women before me successfully and gracefully filled their buckets and were on their way.

My turn came and I strode forward thinking, "this cannot be difficult". I tied on our bucket and let the rope slide smoothly through my hand. Smiling with pride I looked to Martha who nodded at my quick study. Now, to pull it up. No problem, I was sure. I leaned over a bit to center the now full and surprisingly heavy load and started to pull. With the impatience she had warned me against, I tugged at the rope and we all heard the echo of the crack! Wood against rock followed by the full splash from the water base. My first day of chores and I had humiliated myself. I turned and looked to Martha for help.

As always my steady sister was there, patient and kind. She quieted her spiteful friends and simply took my hand and held it in hers as together we slowly pulled the bucket up and carefully untied it from the well rope. I humbly followed her home a few steps behind looking back to the women who, like a herd slowly grazing, drifted off in separate directions from the well.

Thankfully, women are a forgiving community, and the next day I was given a full audience as I attempted to fill the bucket alone again. As my day's water came up without a lost drop, my success was cheered with sincere encouragement as they decided to welcome me in after all. I soon found the joy that carried Martha through her day. It was rooted in this early morning meeting at the well. Here we shared our triumphs and our sorrows. We prayed together for missing boats after storms and we kissed new babies as they joined young mothers at the well. We teased each other about failed recipes and we traded secrets for successful marriages.

These were the women of Magdala. There were new brides with little experience and wise grandmothers whose experience shown in their tired eyes. There was a woman of great strength who could lift two buckets at one time and a woman of greater strength whose fragile arms could comfort a weeping widow. There was a woman who smelled of the earth and seemed to be connected to its every whim, forewarning us of storms to come or promising healthy crops at harvest. There was a woman whose beauty and grace stopped even small children in their steps to gaze at her as she floated by. There was a simple woman who found God in small things like the greeting of an old friend and a philosopher who sought God in the depths of the human spirit. These were the women of Magdala, and now, I was one of them. Even with my thick fingers that could not slide along the wool without tangling it at the loom and my wondering dreams of travel upon the sea, I was one of them. With my bony arms that had just recently begun to take on the soft roundedness of womanhood and my prominent nose that seemed to point my way through life, I was one of them. We were one in that we were women, and yet, not a one of us was the same. Beauty in each and together, beautiful.

What I discovered to my surprise was that while I thought women talked of silks and spices while walking through the markets, I found that actually, quietly, intimately they were sharing their hearts and souls with one another. Something lacking among the men I had spent my days with before. Even the daily task of fetching water became, in the company of women, a cathartic event that washed clean the errors of the day before and left us fresh for whatever befell us in the day ahead. As time went on, if I knotted my fingers in the loom while weaving, rather than curse my chores and my chubby fingers, I would imagine how I would tell my friends the next morning. I no longer feared making mistakes and so Martha finally had a willing student.

Willing I was, but ability I lacked. Mother had completely given up on me and even Martha's great patience had been well tested by my clumsiness that year. I am afraid I never learned the domestic arts as well as my sister. Furthermore, my secret hope to grow close to my mother was never realized either. It must have been my lack of skill, for my mother distanced herself even from Martha the year I was home. Lazarus once told me that I was my father's daughter alone, for I had his strong features and stubborn will. He would tease me that mother wept over my cradle because she saw none of herself in me even as a baby. Perhaps this teasing had a root of truth, for the more I was around the house, the less I saw of her. She began spending time alone in the kitchen if we were out front or escaping to the yard while we tidied up the inner rooms.

By the time the days grew longer once again, my womanly blood began to flow and I was actually looking forward to marriage. Not only had I learned the great joy of the feminine world I had ignored most of my life, but I had also begun to notice the form of men. Their strong arms and long legs stirred desire in me, and the facial hair I had found so puzzling as a child suddenly attracted me. In fact, my sister and I became quite the astute critics of men's beards. We giggled if a young man's beard did not grow in evenly and we sighed at the men whose beard seemed to highlight some inner wisdom unknown to us young girls. I hoped Jacob, the wealthy trader my father had chosen for me, would have a beard I could brag about.

I was pleased at our first meeting and Martha assured me that no one but her could see the flush of my cheeks as he was presented to me at banquet. He was younger than my father, but much older than I and that bore in me a respect for him. His long beard, not yet touched by grey, lay boldly against his strong chest. I tried to study his face as he talked with father, but I was so nervous I hardly remembered enough to have recognized him in town the next day. However, I felt the flutter of my heart and I could hardly eat when he was present, and so, I decided I loved him.

When the betrothal could become official, Jacob gave me a golden ring to mark our covenant and we began to meet in short interviews chaperoned by my parents. I found him kind and attentive and, in my evenings on our tiled porch, I found myself no longer looking for father on the road to town, but awaiting Jacob's visits. I dreamed of embraces and long conversations over family meals with many children running about at our feet. I was ready.

Chapter 4

I remember the marriage...

As my wedding day approached, I tried to imagine my mother as an anxious bride. I could not. She seemed to me to have always been old and tired, bothered by the noise and commotion of us children, and angry with my father for some injury unknown to me. My childhood held few images of her with us children.

My mother had always cared for us in duty without attachment, even for Martha who fluttered around her begging for some affection. However, the memories of my joyful father sweeping me into his arms and onto his shoulder always brought a smile to my face. I wondered, would my husband be a good father? Would I be as cold as my mother had been? What caused that coldness I often pondered as I saw the tenderness in other mothers? She was never cruel, just guarded, unavailable.

As my wedding crept closer, she seemed the same orderly, proper woman she had always been. It was as if we, the family who made silly comments about my being a bride at the dinner table and who danced around the yard in practice for the celebration, had hired her to fulfill the formal arrangements. There was little joy in her preparations, but she did what was required with Martha eagerly learning every part of the hostess role by hanging on her arm and helping whenever she could. On the outside, I continued to accept mother's distance and I clung to my father for the tenderness I needed to quell my fears. Martha, on the other hand, continued to try to win mother over by being as perfect as she could. I never understood Martha's persistence, it was as father said, "like trying to clear the desert of sand one handful at a time". Even father could not woo a smile from mother without a wrapped gift from some far off place, and I doubted whether they had ever been in love. Looking to my wedding, I wondered if I was in love. Were the stirrings in my gut the stirrings of love of the man or love of the wedding?

The day of the wedding celebrations were to begin, my mother pulled me into the upper room of our house for the "sex talk". Since we had not been very close, this was awkward for both of us. I, a nervous bride anticipating the wedding night more that the wedding itself, longed for some advice. She, this cold, selfish woman who had not fostered a relationship with her children, knew her responsibility, but struggled to fulfill it. We sat on the center mat and looked at each other nervously until, finally, she offered one bit of advice:

"A man is like a snake in the grass. If you are lucky the bite will come soon and be over. If he is potent, a child will come. You must not struggle and you will be blessed. Now, my daughter, let's to the preparations." Quite satisfied with herself, she stood up not noticing, or ignoring, my confused look, grabbed my hand, and led me down the stairs to the courtyard for the awaiting party.

A large group of women from both families met us in the front room to adorn me with scented oils and jewels. Pieces of colorful silk wrapped around me, constricting my movement, but making me feel like a queen and setting aside my new worry about some snake to visit in the night. The women encircled me, all the while rejoicing in memories of their own weddings or dreams of their future nuptials. My aunt prodded my mother into telling us how, in her procession, she had tripped over her long gowns, crashing to the ground and pulling three attending girls down with her. I couldn't believe my mother, whose grace and style were praised throughout the community, had indeed been an awkward girl like myself. For a moment, I saw in her that girl as she allowed the story to be told and giggled at her own folly.

As the story came to an end, my mother said with a shot of bitterness, "If only the promises of the wedding were indeed the fulfillment of the marriage."

I looked to my aunt who caressed my mother's shoulder with her hand and kissed her cheek with an understanding of those words that told of the chill that seemed to haunt my home. However, to me, the mystery remained unsolved and we returned to our blissful preparations. Other women filled the silence my mother had dropped on the group with stories of happy weddings and fruitful marriages. I felt like I was welcomed into the sorority of wives that day. I almost forgot the wedding I had before me and wished only to stay with these, my sisters. However, we were interrupted by a servant who said the guests awaited and I was swept back into reality, ready to embark on my own blessed future.

The party was beautiful, the ceremony memorable, I am sure. However, once I left the safety of the circle of women, all I could think about was the fear of the coming night and the snakebite that caused the blood on the sheets of brides the next morning. As my sister, mother, aunts, and new in-laws arranged my hair and accompanied me into the bridal chamber, I prayed to God that the bite would be quick and the children numerous.

Later, as the years of our marriage went on, I often wondered if, in my haste, I had not gotten the words of my prayer transposed, for the bites with his fist came often and the children would not be born.

It was not long after the wedding week that Jacob realized my clumsiness at housekeeping and my inaptitude at any of the crafts women are praised for. My fingers, still chubby from childhood, tangled in the loom and left my weaving knotted and useless. My cooking was flavorless and usually burnt. My beer tasted dry and bitter. For a while he laughed at my folly, saying he was blinded by the "radiance of my beauty which shut out all his other senses".

I continued to try housekeeping and I wished I had followed my mother around a bit more like Martha had when we were younger. Now, I cursed myself as my bread took on the taste of the desert and my wine soured under lack of knowledge of the vine.

However, in that first year, our love rose above my struggles as we learned to find enjoyment in one another's company. Jacob was gentle with me in our marriage bed and taught me not only to pleasure him, but also to find pleasure for myself in our lovemaking. We spent hours in the evenings exploring one another and seeking new ways to express our love. I felt at peace in his arms and he assured me that my skills around the home would develop with time.

Secretly, I called for my sister Martha to help, but I was ashamed and did not want my husband to know I was getting assistance. The plan was for her to come in the mid-morning, after Jacob left for the market, and help me prepare the evening meal for him. She was always gone before he returned home and though my culinary skills still lacked, the unknowing Jacob began to feel pride in his wife.

Our plot was thwarted one day when Jacob returned home early. The Romans had closed the markets throughout the region and had scattered Jews from any central meeting places after a small revolt arose in Tiberias, just south of us. He came through the door ready to embrace his wife and, instead, found Martha leaning over the cooking fire.

"What is the meaning of this?" He cried as he jumped back scanning the room for me. I was standing to the side of her in the shadows trying to follow her every move and not doing a very good job.

Surprised, all I could utter was, " Oh, Jacob, it is for you. I just can't do it. I can't cook. I can't weave. I can't care for your house."

Shame reddened my face and anger brought a rage from him I had never seen before. He threw Martha out and turned to me in disgust. "I have been so proud of you. I had thought you were my wife and here I find my house is cared for by your unwed sister?! I should go back and demand a higher dowry from your father. I have wedded both his daughters it seems, though I am stuck with the useless one!"

With this he struck me for the first time. His large rough hand that had caressed my soft thighs now collided with my cheek bruising it and splitting my lip. The thick blood ran into my mouth and I was startled by its bitter taste as I realized what had happened and began to pull myself up from the floor. He came toward me again and this time grabbed my unused loom and broke it over my back before I could fully stand, dropping me to the ground, where this time I decided to stay. I cowered with my hands over my head, waiting for the next blow, but only heard the door slam as he left.

As I began to stir, a splinter protruding from my shin was driven deeper by my trying to kneel on the floor, and I cried out in pain. I then realized it had been my first cry, for I was too shocked in his attack to react at all. Guilt filled me as I thought of all that I had failed to do for him and told myself his violence was my fault. Sweeping up the remains of my broken loom, I knew my heart had shattered along with it. I was empty and began to move about the house without seeing it at all. The rest of the evening, in a dream-like state, I followed routine around the house. Finally, I fell to sleep as the sun set and did not dream at all that night.

The dull sunlight roused me from bed early the next morning and I was surprised to see my mother approaching over the hills of our pasture. Martha, evidently, had confided in her when she had been thrown out, and mother had come to look in on me. On her head she balanced a large basket and as she quietly opened the door and let herself in, the smell of freshly cut herbs announced her arrival.

"Mary," she seemed to breathe my name as she examined my battered body, "Look at my baby."

I was shocked by her tenderness as she took me in her arms and allowed me to sob until her cloak dripped with both our tears. She laid me down and went out to the cooking fire. There she prepared balm from Aloe plants bought from Egypt for my bruises, and wine for my rest. She stayed with me for two days, during which Jacob did not return. On the second day I began to come out of my stupor and for the first time in my life, I spoke openly with my mother.

"How can a man be both so loving and so cruel?" I asked despite the fact that I expected a cryptic answer like her talk with me about the snake in the grass. Yet, to my surprise she answered directly and I finally learned my father's failures.

"Man is either ruined by the bile of his passions or the bile of his fury. Jacob, it seems, harbors fury in his heart, my husband carried passion. When I was a young bride I did not understand what made a man stay away from home overnight. That is until I awoke with the sickness that killed my fourth child."

"Fourth child?" I almost shouted.

"It is time you know the truth of our family. You are a woman now, and I see that you will live as I have: betrayed. My fourth child, a son, was struck blind at birth due to the illness your father brought home from the whores and gave to me. The Rabbis left our youngest son out to die, cursed as he was by your father's adultery. Every husband has his weakness: passion or fury. It is the burden we women endure in silence. You will recover and you will learn not to stir his rage."

I turned away from her, not wanting to see the truth of my father, not wanting to believe her bitter tale of men. And I cried until I again fell into a dreamless sleep as the wine warmed my head and the realization of my situation made me weak. In the next few days, I found myself seeking isolation from those who could give me comfort. I went to the well just before sunrise to avoid my friends in my shame. Part of me wanted to cry to them, to be fed by their understanding and care, but the more stubborn part did not want to face my realities in the daylight. I left the company of women and tried to make it on my own.

When Jacob did return after many nights away, it was clear he was no longer tolerating my failures. There was no reconciliation between us, just cold co-existence. He grew increasingly impatient and critical. Rather than the family dinners I had dreamed of, Jacob began eating at the inn in town and coming home only to fall drunk into bed. There was no more lovemaking, rather a brief wrestling in the dark, groping, sour breath filling my nostrils, and the collapse of his sweaty, heavy body when he was finished.

In our third year of marriage I became pregnant. I was sure we would bond once again and that maternal instinct would suddenly make my fingers nimble at the loom and my meals flavorful. But to my disappointed dreams, with pregnancy my body seemed even less capable of caring for a home.

I was in my sixth month of our first child's growth when he lost his patience with me for spilling his breakfast on the floor. When I bent down to pick it up, he kicked me from behind and scowled at me, "Eat there with the dogs!"

I obeyed.

The next morning I awoke bleeding and in the terrible pain of untimely childbirth. We lost her, our daughter, and life with Jacob only darkened. For the next nine years I lived in fear under Jacob's heavy hand. Finally, he cast me out.

"Out you barren whore!" Jacob snickered at me with enjoyment of having received the written approval from the Rabbis that would free him from the bondage of our marriage.

He writhed as if in physical pain upon entering my room, as if there was something lethal in the air I breathed out; as if I were the source of death to the three babies I had lost in our 12-year union. At the time of his declaration, I was still recovering from the last miscarriage and shrunk under his words.

"I will let you be if you only give me time to heal," I cried from the bed once again soaked with blood. "I have failed you and I have sinned against God, I belong on the streets, I know," I whimpered, bowing my head to the man who was only pointing out what I had known was coming from the moment I had seen the blood between my legs.

It was not his seed, but my womb that seemed to be unwilling to carry life. I thought of my mother who had died only a couple of years earlier trying to bring forth another for my father's home, and I cursed the burden of women. My mother's body had been too old and perhaps too reluctant to give birth to another child. But I was young and could not understand my failure except that it must be my fault.

I continued to plead for time to recover and begged that he again call for a Rabbi to come and heal me. I was sure that this time the demon, that obviously possessed my body due to my own sin, could be cast out and I could become a mother. I appealed to his sympathy for we had once loved each other and I could hardly stand, much less make a journey.

He could not wait. I could not stay. We had no more words. I returned, shamed to my father's house.

Chapter 5

I remember my descent...

Having proven my failure as a wife, I had no future ahead of me except in business with my father. However, after knowing my mother's secret, it was hard to trust him at first. When I returned to his home, I now saw him as a man with weaknesses of the flesh and could not see the loving father whose arms had held me so many times in love. Reminiscing over my childhood, I now recognized penitent motives in his attention, and I almost resented these once fond memories. Had my mother forgiven him, they both may have healed, but as it stood he was always an adulterer and she, a bitter shrew.

However, the house without my mother had warmed a bit with Martha now at the helm. The door was open to visitors and Martha's welcoming voice could be heard upon approach filling the long empty air of the home. My father never talked of my mother after her death, but he did keep her favorite shawl carefully folded on the sleeping mat in their room. I wondered if they had found peace before she died or if his sin carried on yet unforgiven. Either way, after just a short time there during my recovery, I decided I would forgive him in case she had not. In a way, it was like me forgiving Judah for the abuse that he wreaked upon me in our marriage. I let go, for both my mother and myself, of the pain of the sins of man; and I opened my heart up to my father again, enjoying his company and looking forward to our return to the market together.

My father welcomed me into the world of men and their business. At the stall in Magdala's market, he taught me to deal, swindle, bargain with men on their terms, and to use my useless womanhood to seal deals. I was the perfect entrepreneur: hungry and without remorse, and I quickly surrounded my empty life with articles of my conquests.

He introduced me to the dark side of selling on Market Street in Magdala. I was taught to tip the scales as I sold grain. I was taught to argue the value of someone's prized sheep if they owed money and had no way to return their due. Father taught me that if they had a herd to give, they had something else too, and to return with but half their possessions was a failed deal. I learned the subtle art of seduction, only to leave without having given any of the promised pleasures. I imagined myself a Jewish Cleopatra. I became cold, ruthless, and wealthy.

The market at home was a smaller version of the great market in Jerusalem. Lazarus and I stood in our stall and sold whatever my father had acquired from his dealings around the region. My brother had never run off from home to chase his dreams upon the sea, but resigned himself to staying on in my father's business even after he wed and had children. Yet, he did not have the keen business mind I had inherited from father, and was complacent to stay in the stall and trade with whomever came by. However, an ambitious seller could find excitement even in these dealings. Many from Magdala did not leave except for the yearly pilgrimage required of men to Jerusalem, so a cunning salesman could sell a blanket of wool from Nazareth at the price of fine furnishings from Rome with the clever tongue willing to sever a poor peasant from his money by feeding his fantasy. There in the market, the clinking of Caesar's gold held a new magic for me. I hungered for its glimmer as it nourished my resentment of failed family life. If I could only gather enough money to fill my house, my empty womb would be silent.

And it helped that men enjoyed doing business with me. I soon learned to recognize their look of amusement when they saw a woman out of place. "Oh, this will be fun", I could almost hear them utter to themselves. They were never modest enough to think I could outwit them. When I saw a deal going sour, I would imagine I was the seductress Cleopatra and exit the stall walking with the image of a swaying desert palm in my mind to present a stronger offer. Hence, the game: the men saw me and thought, "let the woman play in our sport and don't be too hard on her". I, of course, used this to my advantage and knew that if I didn't challenge this belief outright, they would hardly notice when I won. And I did, often.

I spent the next three years honing my sales skills. I collected many a traded item in my room and lay at night watching the moonlight dance off lamps from the Arabs, silk from the East, and gold plated bowls from the Romans. I collected the world in my room and I began to feel I owned it, or as much of it as one could. Because of Lazarus' lack of ambition, as father got older it was I he pruned to take over the business. And what choice did I have? A divorce was easy to recover from if remarried, but why would a man take in a woman who couldn't produce? And if I couldn't produce there, I certainly could in the market.

Soon enough, my father began to bring me on his travels around the region and it was on the road where I truly learned the art of trade. My first exhilaration from a deal came at the price of a widow's strongest sheep. I had watched my father long enough to know that you looked at the goods you wanted to acquire and not at the person who presently held them. We were in a small village outside of Tiberias, just south of our hometown on the Sea of Galilee and my father had already guaranteed a man in Cana that he could double the size of his herd before winter so that he would be ready to produce lambs for the Temple Market at Passover. We were desperate, and there is a certain excitement in that.

We had heard there was a newly widowed woman in need of selling her last possession: the few remaining sheep her husband died defending against a progressing Roman Army. So, I went to her. My father stayed at the inn, feeling that a woman with her feigned sympathies could better strip the widow of the last of her wealth. He prepared me with a basket of sweetmeats for an initial gift, and filled my purse with stones that resembled jewels and foreign coins of little value to seduce the woman's need; a hungry woman with small children is easily confused about the value of trinkets.

As I rode up on my awkward donkey to the adobe home I noticed the door was left open. In the larger cities we had begun to see more closed doors as thieves no longer waited until dark to clear out a home. She must have been comfortable at some point for they had added on a second room in back and an upper room that looked almost new. In the background a manger large enough to feed many animals lay empty. Someone had obviously tempted her into selling her milking goats, and it looked as though she had even owned a camel at one time as the riding blankets still hung from the rotting fence. I rode on toward the house with a confidence I had picked up from my father.

As I dismounted three children peeked out of the doorway, looking hungry but proud. The smallest, a young girl of four or so, stepped toward me with expectant eyes and I felt myself soften a moment, wanting to reach out to her and offer her the meal I had packed for myself. However, just as I began to swell with compassion, the baaing of sheep from the adjacent meadow called me back to my purpose and I was again resolute to give little or nothing to this family. The soldiers their father had struggled against were physically violent, but it was nothing compared to the violence that we traders were capable of inflicting: we gave a lasting loss, which they would feel each bitter time they found our trinkets of trade worthless.

When the mother appeared I felt a different pang: one of jealousy. Why was this woman who had no skill to offer the community able to bear three children and here she stands without the wit to care for them, while I, who was surrounded with comforts, could bring forth none? Now, I decided she owed me. I smiled at her as if I did not see her suffering and handed her a basket of sweetmeats to share with her children while we talked inside. I had found in my trading that if I offered gifts first, clients felt as though they had received part of the payment and were obliged to deal. I saw in her vacant eyes that she already felt indebted as the children embraced the basket.

Entering the home I almost tripped on the fire pit in the middle of the room. I had not adjusted my eyes to the darkness of the thick brick walls, for she had no lamps lit in the daytime, preserving her oil for evening. I thought of the extra jars of expensive oil I had stacked along walls. We had lamps lit all day; we were never in darkness. As my eyes began to focus on the reception room before me, I was startled by a small skinny lamb hiding in the corner as if aware it was to be the next bargaining sacrifice for the family, or its next meal. She had traded away much of their possessions already; this was evident in the indents left in the floor from sold pieces of furniture. Even the bedrolls lay in the ghost of a container, carefully folded and set inside the square markings of some lost box.

As we sat, I began with honey in my words, "I come, sister, after hearing of your great need. For my family is in the practice of sharing whatever we can with our fellow Jews in this difficult time. We travel and see many woes such as yours and only hope to lessen the struggle by trading your troubles for what we can offer."

She looked suspicious of me and I was surprised to see some wit in her at last. I distracted her by dropping my purse on the blanket we sat on, allowing some of my excess coins to roll out. I did not move to search for my lost coins, showing little concern for them. Quickly, however, with an instinct of a worried wife, she crawled to her knees and collected them for me, handing them back reluctantly. I thanked her and continued.

"I see that your children are not yet old enough to tend your flock and wondered if I could procure it from you with a generous trade? You see, we have a young widow up north who is in need of some occupation for her grown son and I see you with this burden of tending the flock with no one yet to help. My thought is to trade these jewels of great value I received from the Roman Governor himself for your troublesome sheep. I am sure you could use the proceeds from these to feed your darling children just as the poor woman I spoke of could give the sheep to her son for his advancement."

She had yet to speak to me and as she spoke I heard the trembling in her voice of a woman who, until now, had left the bargaining to her husband. Oh, how we women need to learn from men their art of survival! I grew impatient, for I had begun to hate this weakness of our sex as I strove to succeed among men. She asked, timidly, trying to be bold, a question she had heard from some man, no doubt, "And what do you get? I see that you give me your jewels and my sheep to another, but what for you?"

If I could have whispered in her ear, I could not have predicted her question so well. "Oh, you are a wise woman," I began, mocking her, "You know the world of trade I believe. Well, have no fear; I am to be paid by the woman up north. A small fee no doubt, but it is what she can manage. As I said, my family's greatest reward is to see our fellow Jews comforted under the Roman rule. We need to watch out for one another, as we did under Egyptian rule, under Babylonian rule, and now under Roman rule. We have no Moses, no King David here, only those of us who remember our duty."

As I spoke, I laid the worthless stones before her so that the thin line of sun breaking through the latticed window glimmered on the seeming jewels. She watched the stones, not me, and her hunger and fear drove her now. She knew we had no savior to free us from Caesar. She had seen the Roman soldiers kill her husband, feed on her flock, take their pleasures with her, and terrorize her children. There was no hope left in her, except that which I offered. It took little more to convince her of the necessity of the sale, and as I climbed onto the riding blanket of my donkey, I felt like Delilah, cunning and triumphant. It had been as easy to sever the herd from this widow as it had for Delilah to cut Samson's locks, and I counted my wealth as I left her standing in an empty courtyard.

The next day, father's hired boys transported the sheep not to a second widow, but to a wealthy man who would pay us 50% more per head if we delivered them to him in Cana. We returned home, content in our mission, to the awaiting Martha who was always eager to hear of our travels. She embraced the station of caregiver as if she were made for it.

A warm meal awaited us upon every return, and I told my sister all I had seen as she helped me unpack my bags.

I was proud of my accomplishments and became more like my father every day. The widow was soon forgotten in my mind, except for the pride I could conjure up with thoughts of how wisely I had played upon her fears and hopelessness. My travels continued with many more successful trades leaving many more poor empty, and I began to see the world like a man: there for my exploitation.

Having come into this world of business, I began to lose the modesty and propriety of a Jewish woman. I imagined I was the topic of gossip around the well anyway, and so, it was easy to forget any sisterhood I had with my own sex. Furthermore, I was no longer presenting myself for the prospect of marriage and with that out of the way I could carry myself with a boldness women rarely displayed in public. Men became objects to acquire, not for possible family life, but to satisfy my self-esteem. Was I still beautiful? Was my fruitless body still an object to be desired? I loved the game of seduction and was soon headed toward crossing the line of respectability. My problem was, I could find no reason to say "no". I was already discounted for any proper relationship; and there was no fear of me becoming pregnant at my age and after so many miscarriages. However, as of yet, no man dared to ask it of me. I think they liked to see a pious lady in me, and they each believed they were the only one who could lure me to the line. Foolish men, I could see in them with sex the same lack of wit I saw in women with trade.

There was a young man named Almog whose face reddened like the coral he was named for every time he passed our stall. Soon, Almog began to bring me small gifts each week when he stopped to feign business and talked only of his admiration of me. I accepted his flirtations as they were sweet and I knew, as young as he was, they were harmless. One afternoon when I agreed to walk with him down to the docks, he suggested my father accompany us as to assure my virtue and I smiled at him saying, "Almog, I have no virtue to guard."

That was the last I saw of my young friend. He began to pass our stall looking the other way and soon his affections were turned to a young girl of virtue. The paradox, I realized then, is that men want a woman to be virtuous, but at the same time, they'll try anything to take her virtue. And so, I learned to feign innocence: a simmering aphrodisiac.

Chapter 6

I remember my first man for pleasure, not marital contract...

Barak, a shepherd from Capernaum, from whose father we purchased wool, was my first love affair. My confidence and callous business sense weakened with every flirt of Barak's earthy green-flecked eyes. His tussled auburn hair beckoned me and danced in my dreams whenever I heard we were headed to Capernaum. In my mind's eye I could picture his coy grin that revealed his unspoken desire; I longed to give in to him and dreamt of his embrace.

Our flirtation came to fruition one day while our fathers argued prices. My father was selling the wool to the Romans and knew that a cut of his profit would be sliced during taxing, so he argued for a lower price since the taxes continued to weigh on our people from the heavy hand of Caesar. However, Barak's father was also to be taxed in the deal and wanted to dilute his loss with a higher price for the transporting of the wool. Anyway, as they went round and round, Barak waved a hand to lure me outside to the pastures.

I followed a bit behind, not sure which way he was leading me and, as was my game, I feigned ignorance of his intentions. I found him under a lone shadowy tree at the edge of a hilly pasture. As I approached I lifted my tunic a bit as if to avoid the ground, allowing my lower leg to flirt with his eyes. I saw as he shifted his stance that I was successful in my seduction and he offered me his hand to help me step on a nearby rock and sit with him. Without a word he brought my hand to his lips and kissed each finger, never losing the lock of our eyes. He drew me in and kissed my lips as I allowed his hand to loosen the scarf about my hair and slowly drop my thick brown locks, following them with his hands to my hips. He played with my hair, twisting it about his finger and holding it to his nose, breathing in my scent deeply as he looked into my eyes. He was much younger than I, but he had a confidence and a charm that gave hint to his experience. As he leaned in to kiss me again, his wandering hand gently untied my tunic and searched out the swelling of my breast. He caressed my curves with one hand and my body shook slightly with his tender touch. At the same time, his other arm cradled my waist and led me to the ground.

We were soon swept away in a moment of pleasure as our bodies moved in the rhythm I remembered from the early days of my marriage. I felt as if one with him and a pleasure filled me as I arched my back and gave into the pure lust that consumed us. As he tensed for a moment and collapsed, I fell back to the hot, dry ground. It was over. The false sense of connection and fulfillment left me as quickly as it had come; and yet, he rolled off of me with a complete satisfaction. I envied him. In me, there crept a barrenness and I tried to shake it off; I was jealous of the cool way he lay accepting his conquest, while I lay there feeling more alone than I had before. Another weakness of women, I told myself.

Nonetheless, it became an unquenchable desire for me: that moment of pleasure, that union with Barak that I could not find anywhere else; but the emptiness after each of our encounters grew as well. I would long for the moment of connection, the burning of his touch; but I was never filled, never satisfied. My thirst to be one with him never quenched. But I offered my heart to him and he swallowed me whole.

Our affair continued and our quiet moments after our encounters became filled with our most intimate secrets as we began to confide in one another. I learned of Barak's broken spirit, much like my own, and I wondered if he could ever love me. His mother had died when he was just a boy, and his father turned to drink and whores in his sorrow. Left to raise himself, Barak became his father's drinking buddy and a student to many of his father's cohorts, thus his knowledge of pleasuring a woman. His pain coming from childhood made his heart more fortified than even my own. Yet, that made me love him all the more. I longed to repair his heart and foolishly told myself of the soul mate he could be if only I could teach him love.

However, each time I felt we had moved closer to one another, Barak would pull back and find a way to cause pain by telling me he was unsatisfied with me or that I didn't love him well enough. My trips to see him became clouded with anxiety rather than anticipation. Which Barak would I meet? Would he hold me and sing songs of love or would he roll away as if I was another of his conquests?

Then it happened. One hot afternoon as I lay staring into the blinding white of the sun, I heard him sigh as if bored and I realized I had become only a plaything to him. He could not love me, perhaps he could not love at all. Even as I retell this now, I ache with the pain of hitting his emotional wall and being shut out forever from his heart.

He told me as he lay next to me in the grass that day that he was getting married and we were over. He said it as he dealt with our business, as a matter of fact, as if what we had shared had been a benefit to both of us, but was now not profitable. He was moving on to a more reasonable arrangement. I lay there welcoming the cold, hard bitterness that started from my gut and slowly crept to every part of my being, and I vowed to close my soul to love or any semblance of it.

I said nothing for a moment while hovering on the verge of tears. At last, I was able to turn to Barak and say, "Yes, it is time you married." I stood, gathered my hair into a knot at the base of my neck, retied my tunic in shame as the truth of our relationship sank in, and turned to leave.

"I do care for you." He tried to hold my arm back and comfort me.

"And I for you. Really, I knew you would go one day. You are like the free bird; you cannot stay with one woman. I hope your wife knows that." I smiled as if in jest and playfully elbowed him in an attempt to release his hold on my arm.

"You know me so well." He smiled, naively believing all was well with us. I allowed him to accompany me back to the house where our fathers were again closing a deal that would make both of them a bit richer.

As we walked he began to tell me about the young girl chosen for him, "You know, I would have refused her but she reminds me of you. You would like her."

I listened in silence, smiling and nodding at this odd comparison; but inside my heart wept. Did he really think by telling me she reminded him of me that it would do anything by tear me apart? Please!

That made it hurt all the more. If he can love one who reminds him of me, why not me? For a moment I wanted to scream at him, if you marry one *like* me, why not marry me! But the sudden realization that he too did not see me worthy of marriage chilled my very soul.

He continued to prattle on about her sweetness and how he would love to have the two of us be friends. I almost fell over at his lack of knowing my heart and had to stop and stoop down to touch the ground, pretending to remove a rock from my sandal, in order to cover my paralyzing pain. As I regained my feet, I smiled at him and said, "Oh, I would love to meet her."

Inside I was scolding myself: He was right, my pride instructed me, this had been a deal that had worn out its usefulness. I would not crush under the rejection as Cleopatra had when Mark Antony returned to Rome and married. No, I was not going to woo my lover back into my arms and lead us both to our ruin. It was over. However, I had now touched that cold satisfaction in myself that Barak had taught me; for a moment I lacked the womanly emotion that fuels the flame of passion and was able to look at love and sex with a logical sense. I was not like Cleopatra, my heroine, I was better. I was colder. I welcomed the feeling and cemented this new bitterness in a mask of confidence.

As I recovered from my heartbreak, I sought other men and soon found myself spending my evenings at the inn, a place solely for men and whores.

I also found wine, and I found that men were as easy to sway as poor widows when wine imprisoned their wit. I no longer spent my days in the stall at the market, but rather sleeping off the wine consumed over deals the night before. Money flowed in the inns and I was there to gather it. The men welcomed a pretty lady at their table, hoping to gain more than a business deal, and of course, I saw an advantage to that. However, it was their gold I wanted, not their love, and therefore, I often escaped with their purse having given nothing of myself in return.

The deals made at the inn were often about the marketplace, but many times, a coy smile and a wink won me anything I wanted for free. It was not stealing so much, I convinced myself, after all, they handed it to me. And on occasion, I did allow their false promises of love to seduce my sexual desire. I craved the moments of ecstasy, but though I embraced the icy bitterness Barak's use of me had taught me, I never fully conquered the regret that accompanied my hangover the next morning. Sometimes I would even tell myself that I was falling in love with the man I spent the night with, but it was only justification for my lust.

Thus was my life the next seven years after my marriage. It was filled with worldly wealth and confidence. Yet, inside I was empty. I continued to feel the womb that denied me a family consume me from the inside, and so I quieted its weeping with wine, sweetmeat, and sex. I longed for something and yet; I did not know what it was I sought. I thought I had everything I wanted: goods more than I had room to store, men who desired me, and friends who entertained me. And then my world was shaken. Jesus came back into my life...a little at first as a trickle, and then a rushing flood of the Spirit.

Chapter 7

I remember our first encounter as adults...

One scorching late afternoon, as I was recovering from yet another hangover on the cool tiles of our seaside porch, my father returning from market announced that Martha was getting married and we all were moving to Bethany. Martha squealed in delight, and I embraced her; however, my hug was as much in fear for her as it was congratulatory. For her marriage, as mine had been, was a business deal, and my father and I were promised a lucrative partnership in her father-in-law's trade business near Jerusalem. Great for business, but who was the groom I asked, jolted into clarity by a protective instinct for my sister.

Father rolled his eyes and answered me, "Ronen is his name and I hear he is the joyful song his name promises."

"I hope he sings of joy and not rage," I warned, reminding him of his choice for me.

He brushed me off and took both Martha's hands and continued his song of praise, "He is wealthy and strong. Handsome, I am told by the women in his family. And a good boy to his father. The two of you will make a wonderful couple."

Martha giggled and was instantly swept into a current of love for this unknown man that carried her swiftly through her year of preparations for the wedding. As the day approached, I was busied with packing up the materials from our stall that we were taking with us and successfully avoided the wedding commotion. Secretly, I was relieved to be excused from the chatter of giggling women as they adorned the bride and told silly stories of long ago. What had I found so attractive in this folly when I was young? Well, that was long ago and I was detached from any joy in marriage unions. Instead, in the last days up north, I chose to spend my time with my brother Lazarus who had decided to stay in Magdala. He was settled there and could comfortably carry on in the market without much trouble.

The wedding week came and went with an exhausting celebration, and I was glad to begin our journey south along the refreshing Jordan River toward Jericho and then up to Jerusalem. It was a familiar voyage and so I was able to mark our way counting off days as we went. All the way my father told me of his plans for a stall in the market during Passover Week: a year's profit in a week according to him. As I listened to his plans for riches I remembered the great market and the flood of people from every providence I had loved as a child. My imagination filled with the goods I would collect and the success we would see there. Just as we started to see the large city with the Temple Mount standing above its towering homes and buildings, we turned off the familiar road and headed east to the smaller village of Bethany.

Bethany was very different from my home in Magdala. It was smaller than my hometown but near the magnificent Jerusalem and only a day's journey to the river Jordan. I took every chance I could to go to the river, as I missed the water of home. Our house was a grand two-story adobe with an expansive walled-in yard. However, there were no tiles to cool one's feet in the evening and no sea to cast the occasional breeze. It was hot. Martha and Ronen lived just down the street a bit and I was happy that I would be able to see my sister often. However, with a home of her own to run, she seemed as occupied as my mother had been whenever I went to visit.

Soon after our arrival, we started in the market at Bethany, and Ronen introduced us to one of his colleagues to help us out with the necessary contacts. Ronen proved to be just what my father had promised: a kind and loving husband. I was happy for Martha and began to relax my protective shield around myself as well. The people of Bethany were welcoming and since we were brought immediately into the business culture of the area, I felt in safe company among the men just as I had at home. However, this was a mistake; these were not my loyal friends of many years. And since I had begun to trust Martha's husband, I projected that good will and gentle humor on the men I knew from the market. I let my guard down and allowed my pride to trick me into false security.

One night, after just a few months of working, I joined them at the local inn as I often had the traders in Magdala. It was a much larger inn than we had in the small northern towns since many who traveled to Jerusalem stayed in the towns surrounding it when its inns there filled. As we entered I stopped in the doorway, startled by the many Roman soldiers drinking and eating the kosher food along with the Jews. I was shocked at the Roman compatibility at night with those they oppressed by day, but wine can be the great equalizer, so it seems. As I fell into a great number of cups of wine, which had become my habit, I found myself the topic of conversation among my companions from the market and some Roman Officers. It seems the officers had mistaken me for a whore.

"A whore?" I slurred in my defense. "I am a business woman, a trader of goods, just like my companions."

This response only brought laughter and I struggled to my feet to continue to defend my honor. One of the soldiers steadied me and bellowed to his comrades, "Yes, and it is an exchange of goods we want to negotiate." As he held me standing, he thrust his pelvis into me to emphasize the "goods" he was talking about.

I turned back to my new friends who seemed to have disappeared and suddenly found myself encircled by Romans. My next protest was met with a slap across the face as I was flung like a rag onto a table. The man who had begun the assault took me first while two of his soldiers groped at my breasts and held me down for him. To stop my protest, a large, dirty hand silenced my voice and stopped my breath. I felt the thrust of the soldier entering me, tearing my flesh as I tried to cry out; but the hand over my mouth slammed my head against the table and I passed out. I don't know how many of them had their pleasure before I found myself lying on the street outside, unable to move or call out.

I would have died there but for the mercy of the friends who had abandoned me. For while they were too afraid to risk their throats for a woman they hardly knew, at least one of them did have enough heart to go to Martha's home for help. Her husband gathered my broken body into his arms and carried me to their upper room. There she cared for my body, but scolded my soul for such foolish pride that would put me in a place for men and whores.

"This is why we women are protected by the

rules of propriety. This is where your constant rebellion has gotten you. Whoever heard of a Jewish woman entering such a place?" she began each morning.

My father refused to see me, and so, I was left to Martha and her servants.

For two weeks I lay in bed recovering from my body's abuse. Though I bathed nearly every day, I could not get clean enough. I scrubbed, but still the handprints of the men who had assaulted me stained my flesh and burned my very heart. My one relief from Martha's scolding was Ronen, the sympathetic man Martha had wedded. He was silent, but his eyes carried compassion as he brought me fresh water each morning before he headed to town. He was not active in my recovery, no man could be in my condition, but I heard him often soften Martha's mood before she entered my room, and I knew he, at least, did not wholly blame me. Over time, Martha began to comfort me rather than scold, and one day I asked her who had come to fetch her that night, who had saved my life.

She stopped her busy straightening of sheets and changing of wash water and looked at me recalling, "You know, I hadn't really looked back on that, but it was a bit strange. It was a man I've never seen before, and he did not even knock at our door. We were awakened by him standing in our sleeping chamber. Now that I think about it, I wonder how he got in. We were so rushed we did not even ask. And he carried a lamp that seemed to set a glow about his robes but not the room. I remember stumbling in dark shadows to find my sandals, but I could see his face clearly. Hmm, strange, isn't it."

"Did he tell you his name? I would like to find him and thank him."

"No, I don't remember him speaking at all after he roused us to action. In fact, I did not see him again after he led us to you. He must not want to be found, Mary, that was such an awful mess; he may not want to be thanked."

I often wondered about that man, and it was not until years later when I, myself, saw an angel, the glorious messengers of God, that I made the connection and remembered Martha's description of this encounter.

Slowly, I began to recover, and when I was well enough to venture out, I offered to get water from the well for the household. Martha would not hear of me leaving the house without escort, and so, encircled by whispering, shy maids, I headed into town. Thankfully, by then the gossip around the well had begun to drift from my disgrace to a stranger story of intrigue.

There was a man in the Judean wilderness that cried out with wild words about a Messiah. They said he ate locusts and honey and wore a camel hair tunic. Crazy is right, I thought, thankful this colorful character had shifted the focus from my rape. This community around the well, which had shown such wisdom to me at one time, now made me feel cold and arrogant. Petty gossips, all of them I decided. I hardly listened until they began to tell of how this strange man cleansed people of their sins in the Jordan River in preparation for this Messiah he proclaimed. It was not the Messiah that caught my attention, but the cleansing part; and I instantly vowed to see if he would, if he could, get me clean. He may be crazy, but I felt completely out of control and I was willing to put my fate in the hands of just such insanity.

It was a few days later when Martha was calling on an ill neighbor that I saw my opportunity. She would be gone for at least two days and would take all but one of her maids. The young maid she left behind was easily bribed into silence and so, I ventured out of the house and down toward the river. Traveling alone, I wavered between fear of being unaccompanied and the compulsion to be cleaned of my shame. In the end, the fear of another attack was overcome by the need to rid myself of the one that continued to haunt me.

When I reached Jericho and crossed the river, I saw him standing on a rock. They had dubbed him "John the Baptizer". He did look crazy and I questioned my own sanity in listening to the gossips at the well. However, I longed to be plunged into the river; whether it was to cleanse or to end myself, I did not know. I stood in line behind poor disheveled travelers and spoke to no one as I watched the procession of meetings with this peculiar stranger. When my turn came, I approached him silently. In turn, he said nothing, but looked into my eyes, placed his calloused hand on my head and thrust me downward with a force that took my breath away. The water rushed over me as his hand became a vice upon my head. He was drowning me and I surrendered to the helplessness I felt. I sank into the sorrow I felt when Jacob kicked me out. I swallowed the wave of pain of Barak's rejection of me to marry another, I choked on the filth of every man I had taken to bed, and as I struggled upwards only to be plunged in again, I was saturated by the memory of the rape. I fainted as he released me.

A few of his followers carried me to the bank, and as I roused, I saw a familiar face gliding toward John the Baptisizer in the water. I sat up and squeezed the water from my long hair trying to decide where I had known this face. Was it a man I had bedded? Afraid that was it and that I would be recognized, I hung my head low and watched through strings of wet hair.

The man approached the crowd and John cried out for all of us on the shore to hear, "Here is the Lamb of God who takes away the sin of the world! This is He of whom I said, 'after me comes a man who ranks ahead of me because he was before me.' I myself did not know him; but I came baptizing with water for this reason, that he might be revealed to Israel."

I sat watching as the two men embraced each other and the new comer said, "Cousin, I come to be baptized."

John looked shocked and challenged the man, "Jesus, I need to be baptized by you, and do you come to me?"

The man, Jesus, replied simply, "Let it be so now; for it is proper for us in this way to fulfill all righteousness". As He spoke, I recognized His voice and, parting my hair from my eyes, I strained to get a more clear view of His face.

He turned my way to look to the crowd on the shore and at once I knew who he was as I uttered, "Jesus of Nazareth. I know you." It was the boy we knew from the market, but He was now a man. It had been many years, and I was relieved that He would not know me when I realized the state I was in, dripping from head to toe and sitting in the sand, a grown woman, a shamed woman.

He now addressed the crowd and John echoed what He had said, "Let it be so now; for it is proper for us in this way to fulfill all righteousness".

And so John proceeded in baptizing my childhood friend, and what happened next struck us all dumb. As Jesus rose from the water we were blinded by a stream of light shining down from the heavens: God himself turned His face to us. And then a dove alighted upon Him. The earth below us trembled and the waters quaked with the booming voice that penetrated us and seemed to come from everywhere, yet nowhere discernable, declaring, "This is my Son, the Beloved, with whom I am well pleased."

The crowd closed in around Him and praised Him, falling to their knees as John continued his litany of prophecy that this was the Lamb of God who takes away our sins. I sat cemented to the sandy shore not sure what I was witnessing but certain I wanted to share it with Martha. Martha! Suddenly, I remembered my transgression to my sister's rules, and I gathered my sandals and hurried back toward the house.

When Martha came home, assuming I had been in bed the last few days, she told me the story from the women at the watering well about Jesus. She asked me, "Do you think it could be that boy Lazarus used to play with? She said he was from Nazareth, isn't that where that boy was from?"

Hiding my knowledge, I discouraged her, "Martha, that boy was a carpenter's son. What would he be doing here at this time of year?"

"You are right sister," Martha consoled herself, "Tales do grow by the water of the well."

Having successfully hidden my witness of the extraordinary event, I vowed to put it behind me, for it grew dimmer as the days passed and I began to question if I had witnessed anything at all. I felt myself stronger and I wanted to return with my father to my business and to my normal life.

Chapter 8

I remember our second encounter, a wedding feast in Cana...

After some time and some prodding by Ronen, my father was able to look at me again. Even after I moved back into his house, however, his disappointment and shame kept him busy or in another room; but eventually, his greed and perhaps loneliness in business brought him back to me and we returned to the market together.

Our routine of the day echoed that of my childhood. We walked to market together in the morning talking of all the great deals we would make that day and I spent the entire day folding materials and cleaning the stall. It had not been spoken, but we both knew I was not yet ready to actually negotiate trades, and so I played the role I had so very long ago. I enjoyed the simple tasks I returned to. I sorted material by color and then by the region in which it was woven. I hardly made eye contact with any of the buyers and many mistook my awkwardness for modesty and complimented my father on his lovely maiden daughter.

Oh, if I could only return to those days. Could I erase my mistakes and start again. No. Forever I would be stained, tarnished not only by the rape, but also by the sins I welcomed into my life. I had created my own Hell with my lust and now, I felt the baptism had washed away any desire of the flesh within me. However, I did not turn from sin, only changed variety: for comfort, I turned to my material good. The market would be my comforter, my goods would be my confidant, and my wealth would be my lover.

I did not want to be close to a man. I did not want to love again. I found myself protecting my heart and my body from any intimacy. Was it fear or repentance? I was not sure, but it was easier to bury old wounds than to risk creating new ones. As always, the hustle and bustle of the market offered diversions that allowed me not to think too much about my own issues.

There was a new trade in Bethany that year. The Romans, tired of the upheavals in Jerusalem, detoured their slaves through Bethany after crossing the Jordan from the East on their way to the great port at Caesarea. From Caesarea the slaves would be loaded onto ships, which they rowed themselves, and brought to Rome for the games that entertained the Emperor. A ghastly sport I had heard. Men fighting men to the death, or when bored with that, the Romans threw the unarmed men in with beasts: lions, tigers, wild dogs.

At first, as they passed through Bethany, I watched the men chained together, heads hung in slow procession, with detached amusement. They were of all colors, such as I had seen at the port as a child; however, their arms were scarred and their spirits broken. Once you see a man who has lost his spirit, you never forget that vacant look, much like an animal, staring at you from an empty living carcass.

One day, as I was watching, amusing myself by making pictures out of their scars, I realized that I stood as they did, staring at the ground as I walked. I got up from my spot on a stack of unsorted crates of goods and tested my posture against one of the posts of my stall. I could stand upright and look forward, but it felt unfamiliar, and as I allowed my body to relax, my shoulders slumped forward, my spine curved and my eyes fell to the ground. I looked again to the gladiators. Large chains of metal forcibly curved their bodies and wrenched them almost into the ground as man dragged behind man, each causing another's pain.

Knowing full well what my own chains were, I stood erect refusing to be held down by sin and violence. And for the next several days, I forced myself to look people in the eye, meeting the world again with pride and self-assurance. It was only then, when I had reclaimed my own connection to humanity, that I began to feel sympathy for the men in chains. I now looked to their scars and winced, rather than imagined. I strained to make contact with their eyes, hoping for their sake they could find a bit of their souls within themselves in the reflection of another human's eye. It was not their poverty and slavery that made them lose their humanity. It was we who stole it from them as we turned away from them in disgust. The Romans abused these men as they had abused me and I hated them for it. When my father announced we had a trip to make to Cana, I was relieved to be leaving these sad men, but I also wondered who would look them in the eye while I was not there.

My father and I had been invited to the wedding feast for the son of the shepherd whose flock we had doubled a few years before. Out of gratefulness he wanted to share the wealth we had allotted him in our dealings.

My father and I had not traveled together in a long time and it allowed, or forced, us to talk. The first night we kept to the shallow talk of trading and wealth. But on the second night as the fire glowed between us and the night grew silent, Father came and sat beside me, handed me a cup of wine and said, "Mary, it is time we talked."

"We talk all day long Father, what do you mean?"

He shook off my avoidance and looked me directly in the eye to say, "I am sorry Mary. Sorry I introduced this world of business that has made you so vulnerable. I am sorry I did not come and take you out of the inn as your sister begged me to before such great harm came to you. I am sorry my daughter, my love, that I could not protect you."

"Father," I began so unprepared for this confrontation, "there is nothing to be sorry about. I took my own road and I made my own decisions. It was the violence of the Romans that none of us could have foreseen. I am the one who is sorry for bringing shame on the family."

"No, No my daughter", he began but his weeping overcame him, and together we spoke no more, but forgave and released our pain into the night. In his arms I again became the daughter whom he carried on the road to market. And we continued our journey once again father and daughter.

We arrived in Cana renewed in our relationship and ready to celebrate. It was a beautiful wedding. Though weddings still rang of dread to me, I was able to enjoy the festivities and being among people who, I assured myself, knew not of the attack.

We stood outside the groom's home, and I saw him, like a king adorned with the finest clothing and a gold crown purchased from the Far East. Even under another's rule, Jewish men could be king for a time during their wedding. It reminded me of

Jacob on our day. The joy I had felt when seeing him dance down the road to take me from my parents' home has never been equaled in my life. Today's bride was lavished upon with jewelry and perfume as I had been in my youth. As the procession passed me, I found myself in a secret prayer that she bear numerous children, safely. Surprised at my sudden sympathy for my sex, I turned to get a drink of wine and quiet my memory.

The party went on for days before I noticed the man from Nazareth in the crowd. I watched Him silently from afar, a bit afraid of Him. Further, I did not want to be reminded of the amazing spectacle I had seen at the river since I was still grappling with what I had witnessed, what I had heard. And then I saw her, standing at his side, his mother. She looked older, but still had the tender spirit that carried grace in every move that I remembered from my childhood at the temple. I forgot any of my motives to avoid Him at once. I quickly excused myself from the group of men with whom I was presently flirting and almost skipped up to her. As I approached, the confidence of my adulthood sloughed off of me like a heavy skin and was replaced by the childish desire to be righteous in her eyes.

She recognized me at once, "Is it Mary, my little friend from the Temple Courtyard?"

I embraced her, unable to say anything and she seemed to awaken a pain so deep within me that I had thought I had buried it forever. She and I stepped away from the group and with motherly love she stroked my perfumed hair and pushed back my dangling bracelets to hold my bare hand. She noticed my pain and met it with empathy. As we walked away from the crowd, Mary kissed my pouring tears with my trembling hand in hers. She did not ask for explanation, she only offered consolation. Drenched in wine from the feast, I wept as she continued to brush my hair out of my eyes. I was suddenly aware of the heavy odor of my perfume and my costume-like appearance as I sat with this modestly beautiful woman in her simple frock and unjeweled arms. I knew that she could see through the jewelry I draped about myself like the heavy chains of the slaves. I knew because she was a woman and we women feel one another's hearts, we see the woman and not the decorated casing men adore. I felt no judgment in her arms, only love and the sisterhood I had rejected in my own community of women.

Once I had recovered my decorum, she tried to politely complement my apparent wealth though she brushed the bangles on my wrists aside as if they were worthless toys in the way of the bonding of our hands. She softly assured me, "You must be doing well, Mary."

"No, I am ill, dear Mother of Jesus. I am weak and I am ill."

"Come to my Son, sweet child, come to Him", she soothed my sorrow and brought me over to my childhood friend, Jesus. I resisted, but she gently guided me and I could not refuse her. As we came closer to Him, she whispered, "Follow my Son, He can heal your pain. As Isaiah told us, 'a bruised reed he will not break, and a dimly burning wick he will not quench'".

I was startled at her reference to Isaiah's prophecy of the coming Messiah and was about to question her when He looked at me. His eyes penetrated my heart with the same kindness she had used to comfort me, and at once He knew who I was. I don't mean the girl he had seen in Jerusalem, I mean He knew who I was now. He saw the conquering Cleopatra I had become and His dark brown eyes invaded the darkest corner of my self, vanquishing the shadows where I hid my secrets. Yet, again I found no anger, no condemnation, only light for my darkness. He was like no man I had ever known.

Kindly, He took my hand and said, "It is good to see you again, Mary. I was glad to see you with my cousin John."

He had known I was at the baptism? How? There were so many people and I had stayed on the shore afraid my venturing would be revealed to my sister. "I did not know you had seen me." I stammered, "Good to see you too." I blushed like the virgin we both knew I was not as He led me a few steps away from the others.

"Mary, you were cleansed of more sin than you own. The miscarriages, the attack, those were not yours to burden yourself with. They are not your fault."

His words rang in my ears a moment before my head and heart wrapped around them, "not your fault". He was the first to say or even to believe that and at once they were lifted from me and I was freed. I embraced him and, knowing we had to return to the banter around us, simply whispered, "Thank you."

I turned from Him, still breathless from this encounter, and began to draw the others around Him into conversation. Jesus had evidently come to the wedding to see His mother and His other relatives who watched over her now that Joseph had passed. Jesus also had with Him five friends who called him "Teacher". One of them, an older man, welcomed me with a smile and handed me a beautiful shell he said he had found during their stop at Caesarea. I looked at the shell and then at the gift-giver. It was Simon, the fisherman who always told us stories in Magdala!

"Simon!" I almost shouted in surprise. "I am the sister to Lazarus, the boy who wished to be a fisherman with you in Magdala. Are you still handing out gifts to curious children?"

"Oh yes, always. I remember you, Lazarus' trusty sidekick. However, I always thought it was you who really wanted to sail." He jested as his memory of me enlightened our reunion. Behind him another familiar face appeared, his brother Andrew.

"And he's still telling his tales as well," Andrew circled around Simon to welcome me, "However, his name has changed: He is now dubbed 'Peter'."

"The Rock?" I questioned and I must have wrinkled my nose as they both began to laugh at my reaction to this new name for Simon.

"The Teacher has given me my new name and He tells me He shall build the Church upon me." Peter stood taller as he announced the last as if to a crowd rather than just the few of us. And in true form, he allowed this to be a springboard to a story. Peter danced with enthusiasm as he told how he and Andrew were called away from their fishing to follow Jesus.

As he rambled on excitedly, gesturing with his hands worn from hard work, my business mind began to calculate his losses: walking away from a lucrative fishing business to do what? Follow Jesus? And he did not even know where? I knew Jesus was special, but my experience told me there was no money in preaching, and as I humored Simon Peter by listening to his story, I couldn't help but think he was a fool. Suddenly, we were interrupted by Mary returning to the group with the wine steward.

"They have no more wine." Mary whispered to Jesus, but we had all quieted our conversation in curiosity. His disciples looked on expectantly.

"Woman, what concern is that to you and to me? My hour has not yet come." Jesus answered in a confident, yet corrective manner.

Mary, with confidence of her own, a confidence in Him, turned to the steward and said, "Do whatever He tells you." Jesus smiled at His mother, knowing He would do want she wanted Him to: she was, after all, His mother.

I stood a bit confused wanting to offer my father's service. We were in trade and could probably sneak away to town and barter for some wine if needed, but I was struck dumb by the odd transaction happening in front of me, seemingly a common occurrence in the presence of this man from Nazareth.

Jesus turned to the stewards who were as baffled as I and said, "Bring to me the purification jars." One of the stewards started to question Him, but decided against it and returned with the others carrying six thirty gallon jars.

Jesus ordered, "Fill the jars with water." And they filled them to the brim, mumbling to themselves about this being a waste of time, but He continued His directions, "Now draw some out, and take it to the chief steward."

So, they took it. I could see their hesitation, as they too did not know how this would solve the problem of no more wine; but they did as they were told without uttering the question that hung in the air. I followed, with the same curiosity that drove me as a child, and heard the shock in the chief steward's voice as he said, "Where did this wine come from?"

"Wine?" shrieked the surprised stewards.

"Yes, fine wine indeed. Quick, bring it here and we shall serve it to the honored guests." He found the groom and pulled him aside, instructing the young man in his error, "Everyone serves the good wine first, and then the inferior wine after the guests have become drunk. But you have kept the best wine until now."

The groom, drunk as much with wedding bliss as with wine, brushed off the haughty teacher of etiquette and continued his dancing. I stood staring, not sure what I had seen, leaning against the trunk of a tree for stability.

I enjoyed a cup of the excellent new wine myself, and I still could not believe that it was water just a few moments before. Who was this man from Nazareth with whom I had run and played as a child? Puzzled and perhaps afraid, I watched from afar the rest of the wedding week and ventured only as close to Jesus as my conversations with his mother and with Simon Peter.

Chapter 9

I remember our third meeting, at last I knew Him...

It was not long after the wedding feast at Cana that Passover occurred, and this time father and I were to have a stall in the center Temple Market selling doves for sacrifice. I was thrilled. Here was an opportunity for me to get fully back into selling and to do it in one of the largest markets in the region. This was our first spring so near to Jerusalem, and I looked forward to participating in the market I had enjoyed so long ago. This time I would not be an observer at the fringe of the open courtyard of the temple, but I would be in the midst of the moneychangers and sellers of goods.

We filled our cart with doves and headed to the city a few days before the flood of Jews was to arrive. Setting up, I became intoxicated by the participation in the great ritual of the Temple Market. I looked forward to bargaining with worshipers and collecting a year's profit, as my father had promised, in this one week. We settled for a stall next to the sheep sellers despite the smell because they had procured a central site nearest the entry to the inner courts. Immediately, however, the market looked different to me. As I spun around to admire the beautiful stonework of the courtyard, my heart grew heavy at the sight of Roman Guards atop the colonnades. From their perch they loomed down over us Jews like vultures, watching for any sign of disturbance. I hated them for the way they looked at us. I hated them for their very presence.

A young girl helping to herd the sheep in next to us, snapped me out of my bitterness, and I smiled at the thought of her here in the market as I had been at that age. Her dreamy eyes engulfed every sight as she peered passed her work to the great sea of goods in front of her.

"Hi," I offered in welcome, "We women need to stick together in this place." She smiled at being included in the category of "women" and I continued, "I am Mary, from Magdala, and you are?"

"I am Ruth. I am father's only living child as there is a sickness up north. We are from Magdala too. Where do you live there?" She shared a bit too much as children often do when in conversation with a stranger.

"Well, we now live in Bethany, but I grew up there. Tell me, what is this sickness?"

"Some say it is a plague. Others, a curse because of our dealings with the pagan Romans. I just know it took my brothers and my mother, and I fear my father soon." She studied the ground as she shared this part.

"Well, he looks fine. Healthy, in fact." I tried to console her and decided I better change the subject before the apparent swelling of tears overflowed onto her cheeks. "You will enjoy the market. It is a place of spectacle and wonders. If you would like, I can share a few stories I heard here when I was your age."

"I would like that very much. Thank you." She almost whispered as her business minded father came around the corner and beckoned her back to her duties.

Oh, I would enjoy sharing Mary's old stories, and to a girl who is learning the market just as I had done. This will be some festival, I told myself.

Then they came: the Jews poured through the gates with money eager to crawl out of their purses into ours. The first day I sold a fourth of my doves and father had to go and try to trade for more for fear we would run out before the end of Passover Week. So, with him gone, I took over the stall quite comfortably and began to bargain with pleasure. What I saw in front of me were not fellow Jews celebrating Passover, but purses full of clinking

Caesars tied to an endless supply of opportunities.

It was late in the afternoon, the sun shone in from between the great walls of the temple streets, making it hard to see people's faces. They were like solid shadows with auras of light. Emerging from one of these shadows I saw a woman approaching whose face looked familiar. I blinked the light out of my eyes and her features became more distinct when I recognized her worn face and nervous hand heading toward my stall to purchase a dove. Then it came to me; she had been my first real trading conquest: the widow whose herd I had acquired with a few trinkets. Pulling her along were two of her three children struggling to grow with minimum nutrition. I pitied her, though I would not allow myself to feel shame that I had anything to do with her state. The woman did not recognize me, but the look from her young daughter told me that this child knew who I was. The brave three year old who had charged out the door to meet me was now near ten and she began to pull her mother to another stall when I drew the woman in with a promise of a good deal. The young girl scowled, but the mother evidently did not remember me.

I knew my profits were great this week, and I don't know if it was sympathy or the guilt I was fighting off, but I convinced myself that I could afford one dove for any trinket she might offer. I held out a dove and she reached out to me with a small coin. As our exchange was about complete, our hands were shattered by the crack of a whip and we both dropped our treasure to look up and find a man glaring at our transaction, whip readied in his hand.

I was in shock. It was Jesus. What was He doing?

There He stood in the center of the stalls, "Take these things out of here! Stop making my Father's house a marketplace!"

His rage echoed against the colonnades and the entire crowd silenced within the temple. As He charged over to the moneychangers table I could not believe this was the gentle Jesus I had known. With a swift hand He overturned their tables and coins flew everywhere. Too stunned to move, the changers allowed the coins to clang against the stone ground and roll in every direction. He had our attention and He was not going to stop.

With His next breath, He turned and grabbed the gate of the sheep stall and freed the animals, prodding them on with the whip still in His hands. Poor Ruth began to cry as her sheep ran aimlessly from her. Next, was my booth. As He neared, He looked into my fear-filled eyes and commanded, "Stop selling these doves in my Father's House".

I shuttered as His voice vibrated in every corner of my being. I immediately abandoned my post and fled as the other sellers were doing, leaving stalls and animals to His wrath. Truly, this was no ordinary man, He had the strength of God in Him and we all felt it. This time, I could not ignore the signs I had seen: this voice I now heard coming from Him was the voice I had heard at His baptism; I had tasted the wine at the wedding; I had looked into His eyes and seen my own soul; and we had all heard of His teachings and healings around the region. I would do as He bade me. And, oddly, rather than avoid Him in embarrassment, I was now driven to seek Him out. I was determined to hear Him teach this week.

When my father learned that I had abandoned our doves, he threw my small purse against the wall of the inn and shouted, "What does this teacher of stories have to do with our profit? Do you know how I had to bargain to get those doves for the rest of the week?"

I didn't have the heart to tell him yet that I thought the market would be closed for the week and our profits were gone anyway. Instead, I simply apologized and promised to regain any losses when we traveled to Capernaum, our next market. "One could not deny this man, father. He has not the voice and presence of any teacher, but of *the* Teacher we have heard of."

"He is a man, Mary. He may be charismatic, but the Scribes will not allow this intrusion into the market."

Father was wrong. However, it was not the Scribes, but the people who put an end to the market that year. Still, the result was the same. We made no more profit. The people spent their afternoons outside of town listening to Jesus speak and came in only for the evening prayer in the temple. There was little bought and sold that year, and yet, we did, indeed, profit greatly.

By week's end, I had decided to follow Him. I found myself offering my treasures to pay the passage of the small group's journey. I saw Peter, who was quickly becoming a trusted friend of mine, and inquired where they were headed next. He told me Capernaum was the next place Jesus planned on preaching, and in fact, He had moved there, to the Sea of Galilee's northern coast, away from his hometown of Nazareth. I told Peter that we were headed there as well to try our luck at that market and that I wanted to join the group on their journey north. He smiled and immediately fell to telling of the wonders he had witnessed – he was an eager evangelist for his teacher.

Peter told me stories of rejection by Jesus' family and friends at home, and it reminded me of the story long ago of Joseph's brothers, selling him because he was only a half brother. Could Jesus' family be so estranged from Him? I shared my comparison with Peter and he quoted the Scriptures in response, "A prophet is never welcome in his own town".

We both smiled and nodded. The more I heard about the growing group of disciples, the more I wanted to travel with them. After an afternoon with Jesus and his disciples, I figured I could go with them and meet father at the northern market by the sea when he got there. My decision was made to go with this growing band of students. However, first I had to tell my father.

"You abandon my stall this week, you disgrace your family, I take you in and give you my business, and this is what I get?"

"Father, come with us." I begged. "I must go. Jesus talks of a light we all have and that we must let it shine so all can see. He speaks of forgiveness and a Father in heaven who loves us."

"I am your father and I say you cannot go."

"I am sorry father," I whispered, "I must. I will rejoin you in Capernaum and help you with the market."

He turned from me and left the room knowing I would not be forced to return home with him. It was the last time I was to see my father.

I went with the crowd as we left the Holy City and headed north. It was a long journey, and as we neared the Northern Region, I sought out my father in many traveling groups, but it seemed he had not arrived yet. I was surprised he had not beaten us here, for we were a slow group, picking up members and losing members as each town passed. So, I wrote him to inquire when he would be coming and to let him know I was seeking him. Martha replied in his place:

Mary, Father will not be meeting you there. He has grown too old to travel alone and Ronen and I have convinced him to stay in the local market. We wish you well and hope you know you have a welcome home to return to after you traverse the world seeking whatever it is you are looking for. Much Love, Martha

Oh, Martha's words bit deeply as I recognized her condemnation beneath her wishing me well. The "too old to travel alone" awakened guilt in me and I questioned whether I should return to the implied duty and rejoin my father in business. I decided to talk with Peter about it. I handed him the note and explained the dilemma I was having in my heart.

"It is quite a loaded reply, isn't it?" he started, understanding right away Martha's intention to call me home. "I remember when I was called to leave my fishing boat and family and join Jesus. This is not an easy vocation, nor does he promise it to be. Let me tell you about His coming to me."

"You told me about how you left your fishing and joined Him in joy." I said, reminding him of his story at the wedding.

"Oh, but I have not told you the story for this purpose. Be patient, Mary. Stories retold at different occasions can have vastly different lessons." I blushed, humbled by his chastisement as he continued, "Andrew and I had just brought in the boat to anchor along the shore and were in the water, cleaning our nets and hanging our heads after a long and unsuccessful day of fishing. Some days we wondered if all the fish were taken from the sea, for our nets only brought up mud and shells, treasures to you kids I remember, but disaster for us fishermen."

I nodded trying to cover my impatience, for I just wanted some advice, but with Peter that always came with a story; so I tried to calm my nerves and listen.

"Jesus, followed by a large crowd, approached and asked us if He could stand in our boat to teach since the crowd pressed upon Him heavily. I looked to Andrew and he nodded and went back to his nets. So, we let the Teacher aboard. I accompanied Him to assure His footing on the decaying wood of our hull and I listened while He taught. He spoke of the dignity of every person, and I was inspired by this idea. When He finished He turned to me and asked that I take him out to sea. I was very tired and tried to dissuade him, but He insisted, and you know how He can be. Anyway, of course I gave in and called to Andrew, 'I'll be back, just pack up the nets, our visitor would like a short ride out to sea.'

"'No, you must bring the nets,' this Jesus says to me.

"Again, I protest, 'we have fished all night and caught nothing, but to please you, I will try again. Andrew, bring the nets and join me, won't you?'

"We went out and let out the nets where Jesus said to. It was not five minutes before Andrew started to pull them out and he called to me for help. As I saw him struggling, I ran over, thinking we had gotten our net caught on a rock or something, but as we pulled it up it tore under the weight of our load. FISH, Mary, loads of them. I had never seen such a catch! I fell to my knees and wept to the Man who commands the beasts of the sea. My hand on His knee I looked up into the eyes that could see my soul and said to Him, 'Leave me, I am a sinner.'

"Jesus smiled and patting me on the shoulder saying, 'Have no fear. From now on you will be fishing for men's souls!' I did not make out what He meant, but I knew I was forgiven of all in my sinful life upon the docks of many cities. And believe you me, Mary, I had sinned: Women, drink, gambling: sailors are tempted by the life of the night and I fell prey to them all.

"As we pulled the boat back to shore, I knew I was to follow Him. However, I was not alone. My brother Andrew and I ran the business for my father and mother, and I was charged with the care of my ailing mother-in-law. You see, my wife had passed in the fruitless birth of what would have been our first child. I was troubled by the thought of leaving them, for my other brothers were not yet old enough to run the boat or care for our parents. And here is where our two stories fall parallel, my dear. I too had to betray my family, leave a lucrative business, and follow Him. We all have lives and families and friends who do not understand our calling. And yet we follow, for them as much as for ourselves. This Jesus is more than we can yet understand, and we have been chosen for reasons we cannot yet know, but here we are. And here you belong, sister."

Chapter 10

I remember Capernaum and my forgiveness...

We continued north until Jesus led us to rest on a high hill near the banks of the Sea of Galilee surrounded by the great crowd of people. As they settled, I sat for a moment looking out to the sea of my childhood. We were just north of my homeland and I felt a comfort being this close to where my life began. The smell of fresh lake water awakened a childlike peace in my heart, and I closed my eyes imagining I was back on the porch with my brother, Lazarus, dreaming of our futures. I had dreamt of marriage and children, of an easy life of luxury, of the sea out my doorway and children's laughter on the breeze.

How different my life had played out. I dropped my hand to the ground and picked up the white sand that had been softened by years of rushing water. How fine and beautiful it was. As I let it run through my fingers I contemplated the times of my life that had beaten down upon me. Maybe they were not to crush me but to refine my soul like the sea refines this sand. I breathed in the clean lake air and remembered the shattering of dreams by the blow of Judah's fists and as I released the breath, I let go of the remaining hurt. Again I breathed in the fresh life giving air and in that breath I gathered the self-hatred that had led me to so many men; breathing out, I released it into the wind and out of my self.

Then I recalled the last year: beginning with the water of my baptism, which had softened the rough edges of my bitterness. And now, as I followed Him, Jesus was polishing and loving my soul into a brand new essence. Peter had been right, it was not an easy road; we were hungry often and we slept on the ground when we could not find a welcome home. Often, as Jesus spoke, I had to face my faults, I could not hide from them and tuck them into dark caverns of my mind. He called them out of me to be examined, recognized, even embraced.

I was no longer the little girl who longed for the market, though I was deeply aware that she was who I used to be. Rather, now, within me, there was a woman just discovering herself, a soul about to be rescued from the darkness. I felt on the verge of a rebirthing, a redefining of who I was. I felt as though I was hatching out of the society-constructed shell that held me in the role written by my past. I was to be freed.

Nestled into the hillside among so many others who were transforming as I was, I turned from my inner contemplation as Jesus began to speak, "Blessed are the poor in spirit, for theirs is the kingdom of heaven. Blessed are those who mourn, for they will be comforted. Blessed are the meek, for they will inherit the earth. Blessed are those who hunger and thirst for righteousness, for they will be filled."

Again I found myself thunderstruck by His words. They were not like any blessings I had ever heard. Blessed are the poor in spirit? I was taught that the blessing was to have a rich spirit. And what blessing did this Man find in hunger and mourning? These words made no sense, they challenged every value I had, and yet, as they settled in my mind, I began to see; for if you are not mourning you do not need the blessing of comfort, and if you are not hungry what matter is it that you be filled?

He continued: "Blessed are the merciful, for they will receive mercy. Blessed are the pure in heart, for they will see God. Blessed are the peacemakers, for they will be called the children of God. Blessed are those who are persecuted for righteousness' sake, for theirs is the kingdom of heaven. Blessed are you when people revile you and persecute you and utter all kinds of evil against you falsely on my account. Rejoice and be glad, for your reward is great in heaven, for in the same way they persecuted the prophets who were before you."

These words added to my spinning self-examination. Was He dumping everything we had learned on its head? He spoke with such clarity that the old standards grew grey. For it is true the prophets were not heralded as kings, and that kings often fall to misery in their greed. I thought of my own life and wondered: was the conversion I sought possible?

I felt a tap on my shoulder and turned to see Ruth, the young girl from the Jerusalem Market and her father. They had continued with us. Starting out from Passover they had planned on traveling with the group as far as the turn off to Magdala, but had continued on to Capernaum, being drawn by the healings they had seen on the way and their fear of the sickness that had swept through their family. I offered them a spot to sit and I was humbled by the eagerness of this young girl. She sought His wisdom as I had sought wealth at her age.

Jesus continued, "You are the salt of the earth; but if salt has lost its taste, how can its saltiness be restored? It is no longer good for anything, but is thrown out and trampled under foot.

"You are the light of the world. A city built on a hill cannot be hid. No one after lighting a lamp puts it under the bushel basket, but on the lamp stand and it gives light to all in the house. In the same way, let your light shine before others, so that they may see your good works and give glory to your Father in heaven."

I heard His words and a great sorrow swept over me. I felt a palpable heaviness quenching the light of my soul. I looked at Ruth and saw the reverent, hopeful girl before me drinking in the wisdom of God. While she shone as a bright light, my light was smothered with my sin and my pain. I began to weep the loss of the child in me who had so loved God and yet had traded her virtue for pride, possession, and passion. Could I reawaken that devotion in myself? Was the light extinguished forever? As I lost myself in self-pity, Ruth took my hand and squeezed it. This little girl comforted me. I could hardly stay seated. She was mourning, she was hungry, she was worthy of comfort and love, and yet, she offered me, in her little hand, the strength of the world. Jesus often said to be like the children and here I saw why, Ruth was selfless and of pure love.

Jesus continued to preach. He taught about anger and adultery; he preached about divorce, oaths, retaliation and hatred of enemies. It became an index of my sins as I recognized myself in every weakness He spoke of. Finally, as the hills began to call the sun to the breast of earth, He tired along with His audience, and sluggishly, the crowd dispersed. Before joining them back toward town, I sought my opportunity to go to Him and ask if I could be forgiven. To ask if I might once again light the candle of faith within me.

However, as I approached the small group of His apostles, the closest disciples, I saw He was talking with a local Pharisee who was inviting Him to dine at his home. I slunk back, knowing my chance had passed and watched them walk toward the house of Simon. I vowed to try to speak with Him the next day.

Defeated for the moment, I returned to town with the women of the group hoping to find rest from the travel and the awakening to my self I had begun that day. As we walked through Capernaum, I took in the sights I had not seen since my trading days. It was a beautiful seaside city and I enjoyed the crowds of people going about their daily business. My sightseeing was interrupted as we passed the market street and I heard my name called out, " Mary, Mary of Magdala?"

I paused, scanning the street of sellers packing up for the evening. As I gazed absently into the market toward the voice that was vaguely familiar, a shot of auburn hair startled me and caused my heart to leap. Seeking a face I felt a long forgotten ache in my gut. Was it him? The man waved and as our eyes met, my fears were confirmed: Barak stood before me. My hands shook and my heart beat against the ribs that strained to hold it in. At once the rush of desire flushed my cheeks and I longed for the temporal lustful love his arms offered.

I managed a smile and brought my hands up to cool my burning head, but neither of us moved toward the other. I wanted to run to him, to find momentary solace in his arms, and I stood teetering between the physical love I had for him and the spiritual love I longed to commit to with Jesus. For a moment I could forget the emptiness that followed the passion with Barak; I could forget the shameful redressing in returned modesty, and I longed for that easy connection: how ever brief. The love that now led my life required complete commitment. It was not easy and it could not be selfish like my affair with Barak. A part of me considered abandoning the difficult task of walking with Jesus, and for a moment, I thought about returning to the tempting road in front of me.

But just as my mind raced through lost possibilities, a woman's arm slithered around Barak's waist and turned him toward herself. His wife. As she embraced him, she looked over his shoulder to me standing alone in the middle of the street. How odd I must have seemed to her: unadorned and roughly dressed from travel. I became self-conscious of my worn look under her judgmental stare and began brushing my hair with my hand. It must not have helped, for she looked relieved I was not a young desirable woman, and she simply led him away. Smiling, I realized how much I had changed and how little, if his wife was still warding off flirtations, Barak had changed. He would never be a faithful lover and I found myself relieved I was not her, though I did see our resemblance, well, at least with the old me. She walked as Cleopatra, parting the crowd with her swaying hips and her adorned body was a temple to all things valuable in this Roman world. As I returned to the path my friends had taken, I thanked the Father for this temptation and the glance at the reality of it that he had given me. I would always love Barak, but I knew now I would never let him in again.

We reached the inn just as I caught up to the other women and I was glad to be away from the open streets. I had forgotten that this was the home of my lost love. The ache I had felt when seeing him now became a heavy stone in the pit of my stomach and I wanted to sleep away all memory of him. Thankfully, on this night we had paid for rooms out of our joint funds as we needed the rest. As I headed toward my room, an older woman named Joanna, touched my shoulder and invited me to join her for evening meal. "Thank you, Joanna, but I am weary and only seek sleep to nourish me today." I replied exhausted.

"Take rest then, Mary. However, you seem troubled, and if you'd like to talk, I will be up by the fire for a while after we dine."

"Thank you again, Godspeed." I held her hand tightly as I bid her goodnight.

I welcomed the soft hay of the mattress and wearily laid down in the quiet of an empty room. As I lay there in the stillness, Jesus' command of the day, "Repent, for the kingdom of God is here" kept running through my mind. As I closed my eyes to rest, I suddenly heard it audibly echoing through the room. Startled, I sat up and looked for the source of the voice, but found no one.

Trying to ignore this presence, I struggled to sleep. No sleep came, but the faces of those I had wronged came back to my mind's eye as clearly as a dream: pitiful, broken, angered, lost. My mind forgot any thought of rest, and instead, I catalogued my sins: the pride I had felt in my business and in my appearance, the avarice I had enjoyed in every deal at market, the envy I carried toward women who could bear children and men who could conquer their emotions, the anger I held onto at the Roman soldiers that continued to rape me in my dreams, the lust I lost myself in with Barak and other forgotten men, the gluttony of my insatiable wealth, and the sloth in which I had laid so many days recovering from the drunken nights at the inns.

Closing in around me the walls of the room pushed me to run outside. I did not know where I was going, but the voice I heard in my room drove me on through town. I found myself stopping a Rabbi on the road who carried an alabaster jar for anointing. I begged him for it, thinking I needed to anoint myself, to fall sick, to die. I told him I was ill and at that moment, by the look in his eyes, I must have appeared so. My hair blowing in every direction from my wringing of it in bed pulling out the memories of my sins, and my clothes dirty from travel and half undone in my troubled afternoon sleep must have shown the demons I carried. I was ill. I was infected by my demons: dying of my sin.

The Rabbi relented the jar and prayed over me. He conspicuously scurried away as soon as he thought I was under control. I knew he saw me as possessed, and, I realized at that moment that I was possessed. By my sins, chained to them in an endless need to satisfy them. As I wondered what to do next, I remembered that Jesus was here, that He could save me, if only I repented. My desire to be a part of the kingdom Jesus spoke of, to be in the arms of my Father in heaven as he promised, led me to the house where he supped.

I found the house door open in hospitality and walked in to find Jesus seated at the far left, the most honored position at the table. Without hesitation I ran to him. I fell to the floor, weeping of my sins and bathing him in my tears. I emptied myself at His feet, unaware of the crowd in the room that had fallen silent with my intrusion. Suddenly embarrassed, I began wiping the tears away with the only cloth I had, my long loose hair. His feet I felt unworthy of, and could not look to His face, and so I began to kiss each foot in turn. The dust from the road made paste with my tears as I tried my best to wash them. And then I remembered the alabaster jar I had carried in, and I anointed Him with the oil. Only later would I understand my actions; at the time I was Spirit driven, compelled to act. Slowly, as I recovered my sense of where I was, I breathed and looked up at Him.

"Mary, you have come to me, finally," He said as the men around Him stared in shock.

They whispered to one another, "Who is this woman?" " What does she have to do with our Teacher?" but did not ask anything outwardly. The host mumbled to himself, "If this man were a prophet, he would have known who and what kind of woman this is who is touching him – that she is a sinner." He recognized me from the markets, no doubt.

Jesus must have heard his mutterings, for He turned to the host and replied to them, "Simon, I have something to say to you".

"Teacher, speak," said Simon hushing the whispering room with a wave of his hand.

"A certain creditor had two debtors; one owed five hundred denarii, and the other fifty. When they could not pay, he canceled the debts for them both. Now which of them will love him more?"

Simon, enjoying what seemed to be a riddle, looked with a smirk around the room of men waiting and, thinking himself clever, retorted, " I suppose the one for whom he canceled the greater debt." A cheer of approval from the group confirmed he had given the correct answer, but Jesus was not finished.

"You have judged rightly," Jesus nodded. Then He turned to me, lifting my chin with His hand so my eyes once again fell into the soft dark warmth of His gaze, and continued, "Do you see this woman?" And, without waiting for reply, He turned back to Simon, "I entered your house; you gave me no water for my feet, but she has bathed my feet with her tears and dried them with her hair. You gave me no kiss, but from the time she entered she has not stopped kissing my feet. You did not anoint my head with oil, but she has anointed my feet with ointment. Therefore, I tell you, her sins, which were many, have been forgiven; hence she has shown great love. But the one to whom little is forgiven, loves little."

At that moment I trembled at His touch as He once again addressed me directly, "Your sins are forgiven. Your faith has saved you; go in peace." He stroked my hair, a comfort He had learned from His mother, and forgave me in His Father's name.

I stood and exited. Walking back to the inn, I was in a daze. He had expelled a thick heaviness from me, and a calm was draped over me like a prayer shawl: light, beautiful, and pure white. The world looked different. Continuing down the emptying street, I noticed each person I passed: I felt pain for one, joy for another, love for each. The sky had taken on the flicker of a dying candle, but the light that shone my way was brighter than the noonday sun. I was a changed person. I was the child whose love for God was greater than my love for anything else, and I realized that He was everywhere. In the eyes of the poor widow who begged at the corner, in the face of the child laughing as he played a game in the street, in each person I passed, each soul I met, there was God. Our Father, and now this man, whom I have heard called His Son: I belonged to Him.

The next morning I rose refreshed and renewed. I drifted to the group of Jesus' followers decidedly and ready to commit myself and all I had to this group and this Teacher. I knelt before Him resting my head on His knee. His hand again smoothed my hair with a loving touch, and He leaned down to kiss me. We sat in silence for a long time together. There was no rush, no waiting for me to speak; rather, each moment was allowed to be its own. With the touch of His hand, I began to understand that my journey of redemption was not complete. My sins washed from me, I now desired to develop the virtues to give me strength against further transgression. His teachings would instill in me all I needed: the humility to replace the pride; the generosity to overcome my avarice; the love to devour my envy; the kindness to drown my anger; the self-control to manage my lust; the faith and temperance to ward off gluttony; and the zeal to escape sloth. With this epiphany, I looked up and said, "Jesus, I am yours."

"Mary, your Father in heaven loves you and We have awaited your coming home." He smiled and together we walked over to our growing inner circle. There were twelve men who served as His apostles; women, including Joanna, whom I recognized from the inn, and I also realized I had known her as the wife of Herod's steward; Suzanna, also well known among those of us in the wealthier circles; and many others traveling from all parts of the region.

Peter came to welcome me, "Mary, how are you feeling this morning?"

I smiled and looked to the ground, a bit embarrassed as I realized he must have been at supper with Jesus the night before. His weathered hand felt warm on my shoulder as he embraced me, and as I met his eyes to give some sort of apology for my behavior in front of all those men, I saw there was no need. He was my brother and he accepted all of me as well.

As we sat on a rock at the edge of the crowd, I told him of the funds I had at my disposal, which I now wished to give to the group. Peter seemed surprised, but unimpressed. "Money, oh I have nothing to do with that, you should see Judas, the finance handler."

He led me to the newest of our group, a man with fierce features and a shrewish disposition. I was a bit intimidated, but he smiled as we approached and shook Peter's hand warmly, disarming any fear I had.

"Peter, I was just telling these men of the kingdom to come."

"Yes, Judas, Jesus' kingdom will last forever." Peter replied tentatively, which I found curious.

"You see," Judas took it as support to his story, "We will not be enslaved any more. We could just do it, you know. I once heard of a revolt against the Romans that almost worked. It was led by a slave, none the less, a gladiator."

"But the gladiators have their strength and they

are fighters. We are merchants and sailors and tax collectors, my friend, how will we stand against the Roman army?" challenged one of Judas' audience.

Peter stepped in and I at once saw his disapproval of this violent interpretation of Jesus' words, "Judas, Jesus talks of peace. Do not rouse them to your war. Let the Lord lead us as He will and when He brings the kingdom, we shall be ready, whatever it will take, we shall offer Him our lives."

"'Our lives', see you do agree that we are readying for a battle. I have heard it whispered that He is the Messiah, the David to free us from our captors!" Judas half answered Peter and half spoke to the crowd he hoped to excite with his vision of our mission.

"Follow, Judas, do not lead." Peter was cautious with Judas and I wondered if Peter had considered this as Jesus' intent or not. I was a bit surprised myself, I had not thought of an actual war against the Romans. I had been waging such a personal war; I had not considered our outward oppressors. "Anyway," Peter continued as he pulled Judas aside, "Mary here wishes to speak with you." He nodded and I jumped in.

"Judas, I pledge all I have to our purpose," I told him as he quietly wrote down the amount without reaction. I wondered. All the pride I held in building this treasure of wealth and neither of my new companions blinked twice as I gave it all away. I was beginning to learn the value of what we were building here verses the value of what I had spent the last ten years compiling.

"That is good. We have prayed for relief and here you are. Welcome." I did feel the chill of his business-like reply a bit. Was he counting the swords it would buy? Judas was not the warmest of persons, and I felt as though he was glad to have my money more than my self. However, I knew it was his job to take care of that part of our crusade and so, I was glad we had him, though I feared his intensity and this revolt he spoke of.

I turned back to my dear friend Peter to accompany him on his morning rounds about the camp. Peter's zeal for this cause poured out of him as if it were larger than himself and his body could not contain it all at once. He was forever talking: reminding the group of what they had seen, asking questions of Jesus to know more and to understand better, and recalling the prophecies of old that seemed to walk in the exact line with Jesus. Regretting that I had once called him a fool, I now longed for Peter's enthusiasm.

He roused everyone who was still breaking fast and announced we were to pack up and be ready to head out to follow the Lord to our next destination. An eager group of students following the great Teacher, we set off across Galilee to spread the Word, or start a war, I was not sure now.

Chapter 11

I remember our tour of Galilee...

As we traveled, jobs were assigned, and though He had many men in his following, Jesus chose Joanna and me to take care of procuring resources in towns as we approached. With my experience at the market and Joanna's dealings with the Romans in Herod's courts, we women were by far the better negotiators. And we enjoyed our bit of business on the travels. Joanna and I would giggle as we came back to the group with food and water that Suzanna, the young girl who joined us, was a flirt and that she helped lower the prices even more than the fact that we were traveling with the well known Rabbi Jesus.

Suzanna had a softness about her; my womanhood had hardened with my sins, but hers was as fresh as the sea breeze. She did not flirt with intent as I used to. Hers was unintentional, unassuming. She simply asked for what we needed in a way no man could resist. Her eyes burned like an ember and her smile made you want to be the reason for her brightness. Man or woman, you were victim to her charms. However, it angered her that we would tease her about using her "womanly ways", and, offended by our glances at one another, she often would raise the price herself to one she knew was more reasonable as proof she was not trying to woo out a deal. Either way, she helped stretch our finances.

It was good to be with women again and not battling in the world of men for my place. Here was the sharing and closeness I had missed. On one of our trips, as we returned with a cart of food, Joanna told us how she had come to follow Jesus.

"Back when you two were still tugging at your mothers' skirts, I remember you, Mary, coming to Herod's court at Caesarea with your parents while your father dealt with the Romans. You sat near your father as your mother came to join us women. From his lap you soaked in the excitement of the men's trade at the port. There were dancers and magicians, silks and spices, animals I could hardly describe – tigers, lions, jackals, even slaves from every Roman regions and even beyond our world."

As she spoke I conjured up forgotten pictures. I

was indeed young when we visited, for I had forgotten I had even seen a tiger until she said the word.

"You had no interest in our women's circles. It was not all gossip and useless talk, you know. No, this is where I was called back to my Jewish youth. We shared the stories of old and remembered the women who came before us: Ruth, Judith, Delilah, Esther: the strong, the glorious, the god-fearing women of our tradition. Each telling enlivened in us a new image of a part of ourselves. Since I had married a Roman steward, and Herod was forever concealing his Jewish roots to fit in with the Romans, I had little contact with other Jewish women until these trading banquets. The Roman stories never drew me in – their women, even their goddesses, were jealous and spiteful, weak and without spirit: nothing to be proud of. I ached for these days when I could bathe in the stories of our people."

I struggled with her criticism of the Roman women whom I had imagined in some heroic light since my childhood. In my mind I prepared a defense, "What about Lucrecia who had killed herself rather than live with the shame of having been forced to betray her husband. What about Cleopatra?" She was not Roman, but came from that same world I held in my mind as magnificent. Suddenly, I realized how much my idolization of Cleopatra had led me down my road of destruction. And I realized that I too was raped like Lucrecia. It then occurred to me that her suicide was not a virtuous, brave act, but a coward's flight from pain. It had been a struggle for me not to give up on my recovery. Death would have been a welcome comfort in the days following my rape. Perhaps this Roman world, with all its treasures, was not worth all the effort I had put forth in trying to be a part of it. Thankfully, these realizations came in time to hold my tongue and I did not verbally argue with Joanna, but let her continue with her story.

"I served along side my husband for 18 years before Herod's demise, and his son, Archelaus, let many of his old servants go, fearing we would tie him to his father's folly of befriending Marc Antony, fallen enemy to Octavian. I remember when Herod had to go beg forgiveness from the Emperor in Rome for this friendship. We were all quite surprised when he returned to Judea retaining his head much less his crown. I suppose the buildings he commissioned kept the Romans happy; he had built many a temple for their gods before venturing to build ours in Jerusalem. He did keep a happy balance between the two cultures in the early part of his reign.

"Anyway, we continued to live in the beautiful port city of Caesarea, and Archelaus made sure we were all quite well off, but my husband did not last long in idleness: he died more of broken pride than of the fever that finally took his life. Once I found myself alone I wished to be home among my family. Thankfully, the Jewish people are a forgiving people, and I was welcomed back to my community. There I found talk of this man, Jesus.

"With nothing else to do, I decided to travel with a few of my neighbors to hear Him speak in Samaria and, finding fodder for my soul, was His at once. There I learned of His reverence for women and His spiritual healing. You see, there were few of us women following him at that time. The men did all of the gathering of supplies. Oh, you should have seen Peter struggle with bartering at the market. Judas chided him almost every day for lost monies. We are much more organized now and our dear Peter sticks to fishing and story telling, his true callings." Suzanna and I laughed at the thought of Peter trying to out-con a salesperson. His truth of spirit did not allow him to veil anything, so a good trader would know exactly what he held in his pocket and was willing to pay for their goods. Joanna continued her story as we recovered from giggles.

"Anyway, the men were off in town and the small group of us left sat by the town well to rest from a hard journey. It was a scorching noon sun that held us to the cool stones around the well. We had not expected to see anyone from the town, for water is gathered, as you girls know, in the morning to assure cool drinks. However, a single woman approached and so we stepped back a bit to give her access to the water. Jesus, however, remained seated on the edge of the well. He asked the woman for a drink as her bucket reached the top.

"'Do you not know what kind of woman I am?' She sneered at him, 'Do you, a Jew, speak to me, a

Samaritan?'

"Jesus only smiled and stretched out his hand for the water. She was startled that he did not despise her, and shrugging her shoulders, she dipped the cup hanging from her bucket into the water and handed it to him.

"As you know it is taboo to speak to the Samaritans much less share a cup with one. One of my companions snickered to me, 'Does our teacher not know the social custom?' I watched silently, wondering the same thing.

"His only words to the woman were, 'If you only knew what a wonderful gift God has for you, and who I am, you would ask me for some living water!'

"The woman looked around at His feet and declared, 'you have no rope or bucket and this is a very deep well. Where do you get this 'living water'?'

"Jesus said to her, 'A man drinks this water and soon thirsts again, but the water I give him becomes a perpetual spring within, watering him forever with eternal life.'

'Please sir, give me that water', replied the woman, 'I would never have to walk this terribly long trip out here again.'

'Go and get your husband,' Jesus said to her.

'I have no husband,' the woman looked to the ground, suddenly shamed.

'All too true!' Jesus recalled for her, 'for you have had five husbands and you now live with another man.'

'Sir you are wise, perhaps a prophet. If you are so wise, tell me. Why do you Jews insist on worshiping in Jerusalem, when we Samaritans have Mount Gerizim right here?'

"Now, here", paused Joanna in explanation, "is why I became a follower. Jesus loved this woman even in her sin, even in her outcast state. He told her that the time was coming when we would worship together with the Holy Spirit. That it was not where but how one worshipped that was pleasing to the Father. He told her He was the Messiah, and girls, I believe Him. And so I am here, following our Lord.

"Soon after I joined the group, we found Suzanna in Nazareth – a town we have not found much welcome in. So young, the call to follow can come to us at any age, I guess." As she finished she took Suzanna's hand and squeezed it with a wink of her eye.

I later found out that Suzanna was avoiding an unfavorable marriage when she dedicated herself to the group. It was marry or leave. So, here we were: three women giving our lives for the Lord. How ever we had come to be here did not matter, we were His now and He called us all in what ever manner we would hear.

When we returned that day there was already a great crowd and Jesus had taken on a new way of teaching. It was not the direct lessons I heard on my first trip with Him, but He had begun to use stories to teach, like in the old tradition. We pulled the cart of supplies we had acquired in town under a tree for shade as He began with his first parable, "A sower went out to sow his seed; and as he sowed some fell on the path and was trampled on and the birds of the air ate it up. Some fell on the rock; and as it grew up, it withered for lack of moisture. Some fell among the thorns, and the thorns grew with it and choked it. Some fell onto good soil, and when it grew, it produced a hundredfold. Let anyone with ears to hear listen!"

He continued with more parables late into the afternoon and as the crowd slowly dispersed to find supper, our small group of disciples closed in for further teaching. The apostles always sat nearest Him and asked many questions, the answers to which all of us drank in with a fervor. Peter, at last, asked the question we were all grappling with: Why had He gone to teaching with parables?

Jesus answered with great patience, "To you it has been given to know the secrets of the kingdom of God; but to others I speak in parables so that 'looking they may not perceive, and listening they may not understand.'"

He went on to explain the Sower Parable to us students, "Now the parable is this: The seed is the Word of God. The ones on the path are those who have heard; then the devil comes and takes away the Word from their hearts, so that they may not believe and be saved. The ones on the rock are those who, when they hear the word receive it with joy. But these have no root; they believe only for a while and in a time of testing fall away. As for what fell among the thorns, these are the ones who hear, but as they go on their way, they are choked by the cares and riches and pleasures of life, and their fruit does not mature. But as for that in the good soil, these are the ones who, when they hear the Word, hold it fast in an honest and good heart, and bear fruit with patient endurance."

As evening fell, Jesus continued to teach those closest to Him. In these peaceful times, the times He was with His friends, He taught us to listen, to receive prayer as much as to recite it. He taught us how to quiet ourselves and to be present with the Father. He reminded us what He meant when He said, "Let anyone with ears to hear listen!" That we were to listen with the ears of our minds, our hearts, and our souls. On this evening He called us to sit silently and be present with the parable of the sower, and so, leaving the group, I found a spot overlooking the sea.

I breathed in and recalled the story I had now heard a few times and held the explanation fresh in my mind. So, I began. I listened with my mind as I recalled the Sower. I allowed my senses to pick up every aspect of the story. Under the smell of the fresh water I could smell the seed spraying from his fingers. I heard the tapping of the seed as some fell onto stone and path; I felt in my hands the rich soil which nurtured the seed given to it; I could taste the richness of the plants and I could see the darkness of the weeds surrounding the forgetful seed and the thorns piercing the vulnerable sprouts. I stayed in this physical manifestation of the parable for a long time, hearing the story with my mind.

I then recalled the story to myself once more, listening with my heart. I felt the disappointment as I watched the seed roll down the path to nothing, I felt the fear of the thorns striking the unaware, and the joy and comfort of the rich soil that could be found for each seed in the words of Jesus. Freely, I allowed the emotions to wreck my body. I cried, my heart raced, I wept tears of joy. And again, I remained in the story, bringing it deeper into my heart.

Finally, I asked the Father to open my soul that I could hear with the very essence of my self. Suddenly, I was swept into the hand of the sower. He opened his palm and as I, a seed, rolled out, I saw the thorns below me, the good soil not far away. And I finally understood this parable for myself. I struggled with the weeds. I had battle wounds from the thorns. As I lay almost engulfed in the tangling vines of evil, I saw the hand of the Sower again. This time He came to me as I called out, and he plucked me from the depths of the destroyer, resting me safely in the rich soil of goodness. Jesus is that hand for us. Here I stayed for the longest time, resting in gratitude for this Savior who, as I opened my eyes, stood next to me with His hand on my shoulder.

He smiled a smile that took my whole self into His and I knew He had been with me in my meditation. As He walked away toward others in meditation, I laid back on the cool ground, fully satisfied. What was it about this man? Who was He? Where were we going? I felt love for Him, but a love I had never experienced. I could not help but think of the other men I had loved. I tried to compare it, but I could not. I did not lust after Him. I did not wish to possess Him as I had my early loves. Yet, there was a connection between us that filled my soul and God was present when I was with Him. I could not explain it. I thought back to my searching for love and for connection with others that had left me so unsatisfied. I thought how desperately I had yearned for Barak, yet, here I was full, this was it: Love! The Shechina, the divine presence, the moment I had tried to recreate without Him. How many of us, I wondered as I lay there, search for this union without bringing Jesus into it? The connection between two people *is* God, and now I knew I was connected, not just with one person with whom I shared a moment, but with all people. Jesus had brought the Father to me and I was one with them, a part of the whole universe while I rested in Him.

As I returned to the present and left my prayer, I heard the Twelve seated around a fire in what seemed to be a debate. I approached the circle of light, unsure I was welcomed until I saw Peter and Andrew who took my hands and sat me between them. It was Judas who was speaking again of war.

"It is possible. I have heard of a great Gladiator

leader, Spartacus, who led his men against the Romans and defeated many an army. He too came from the masses and dared to reach above his station. Look, why else would Jesus be gathering us together as we travel?"

"He has never mentioned an uprising!" John, who was usually very gentle and soft-spoken, almost shouted.

"And why would he bring along the women? Are they also to fight?" someone else cried out from the darkness.

James and John stood up together to face the others, "There will be a kingdom, have no doubt. His faithful shall help to lead it!" James spoke for both of them as if to claim their leadership among the group.

I was shocked that I had not noticed the tension that must have been brewing among these men all this time. As I feared fists were about to speak rather than tongues, Jesus suddenly appeared beside the fire in the middle of the dispute.

"Fools! Have you heard nothing of my teachings? How can I describe to you the Kingdom of God? It is as a mustard seed. Though this is one of the smallest of seeds, yet it grows larger than other plants. It is large enough so that the birds build their nest and find shelter. Remember the Sower? He planted the seeds and He will return to harvest with sickle in hand. Be alert. Stay awake. You know not the day He will return!"

"We are sorry for our little faith, my Lord." Peter stood up willingly taking the blame for them all.

“Oh, Peter, were your faith the size of a mustard seed.” Jesus whispered leaning on His friend. It was the first time I had seen Jesus saddened and it tore at my heart. With nothing left to say, the men dispersed. As I kissed Jesus and headed to bed, I noticed Judas standing at the edge of the now quiet camp, throwing rocks into the silent darkness.

Chapter 12

I am sent home...

We continued with the learning through parables and each evening after the crowd disbanded, small groups gathered around our camp and made fires and discussed the day's lessons. Often, Jesus and I would walk together, avoiding the crowds and giving Him a break from the demands and questions of His followers. As we walked, our bond grew and I found myself sharing every thought, every feeling I had with Him.

One night I told Him that I felt Him present when I prayed, and He said to me, "Blessed are you for not wavering when you see me in prayer. For you see with your heart and believe. I am always with you, Mary". He took my hand and led me to a large rock where we sat down and He continued, "Soon, I will be sending the apostles on a mission. You too will be sent."

"Anything you ask. I am Yours."

"Home."

"Home? I am to go home?" I answered with transparent disappointment.

I tried to take my hand back, but He held firm and answered, "Home is your mission, Mary. God is not only present in the booming voices of men before the crowds, but also, and perhaps more intimately, in the sharing closeness of women. You will find Martha ready and a group of women eager to hear of the Kingdom. You have the parables to share with them. You have the listening to teach them. Go and be with them. Bring them into the Kingdom."

"Yes, Rabbi." I said, and then asked, "How will Martha know I am coming?"

"It will be as I have said." He spoke with finality and I knew our discussion was over. We rose together in silence and as He kissed me goodnight. I felt comforted in my calling, though I still wondered why I had to go home when the others were off to wonderful places. I had traveled, I had experience. I could not help but be discouraged thinking how minor my role was to be.

The next day we continued our travels with Jesus teaching many more parables and bringing many more people to the Light. Jesus said we were to go across the lake to a place called Gergesa. I looked forward to the trip, for while I often gazed across to the mountainous shore, I had not been to the eastern side of the Sea of Galilee. The people there were a blend of several cultures, and even the Jews were very different from us; they were not Orthodox and did not follow many of the dietary laws. In fact, I had heard rumor of their actually raising and eating the flesh of swine. I began to ready for going, but Peter, a well trained sailor, cautioned Jesus against us sailing on this day, saying, "Lord, we will go where you send us, but today is not a day to be sailing. It looks fair now, but I fear a storm with the way the wind is shifting direction."

"We will go to Gergesa." Jesus said and we boarded the boat Peter had acquired for us without further discussion.

Though I loved to dream of the sea from the shore, I had never enjoyed traveling by boat, for the churning of the water turned my stomach. I held onto Joanna, who sang me songs to calm my nerves. We rocked and rolled along the sea, and while the seasoned sailors allowed their legs to sway freely with the motion of the boat, I grew even sicker trying to watch and learn. I sat down on the floor with a bucket between my legs when Peter suddenly called "Storm ahead!"

Standing up, I was hit by a large wave as it broke over the side of the boat, and I was pushed down again. A chill suddenly cut the air and sliced through the openings of my tunic. I grasped onto

Joanna and saw Suzanna who was oddly calm, watching the clouds close in. With water beating at her face, she stood still as if welcoming the weather.

Joanna grabbed my arm and handed me the bucket I had been cradling. Confused, I thought, "I am too scared to get sick now", but as I saw another wave break over the edge I understood what she needed. We were now standing in water up to our ankles and waves continued to pour in as we frantically bailed with our little useless buckets. Often I would toss water out over the edge only to be splashed by the very water I threw as the wind drove it back on deck.

Peter, James, and John tried to steer the boat while the rest of us bailed water. Peter looked about at his lacking crew and ordered Levi, who was clinging to a fishing net in fear, "Go and wake Jesus."

Levi shimmied himself down the rope to where Jesus lay sound asleep and called out to Him, "Master, Master, we are perishing!"

Jesus awoke, waved His hand, in command to the wind and sea, and returned to His seat. The waves ceased, the wind silenced, and we all stood dumb, water dripping from us, our hands hanging heavy at our sides. Only Suzanna who had shown no fear looked as though she were not surprised. Jesus rebuked us asking, "Where is your faith? Suzanna has shown us true faith. Fear not and believe as she has done!"

Afraid and amazed we looked at each other, and

Levi uttered as he caught his breath, "Who then is this, that he commands even the winds and the water, and they obey him?"

Ashamed of our wavering faith, we returned to our sailing in silence until we reached the Gergasene shore.

Settling into port in the country of Gergesa, I felt thankful to be on solid ground again. I leapt from the boat and fell to the sand of the seashore. Suzanna helped me to my feet and we were both startled by an odd sight before us. A huge man, half naked, wild of mind, and dragging broken chains that hung from his wrists stood before us. His crazed eyes captured us in their sights as he foamed at the mouth and babbled words we could not decipher. I held onto Suzanna in her stoic bravery and prayed he would not approach us any closer until the men from the boat had joined us.

Suddenly, he ran around us and fell at the feet of Jesus as He pushed through the water to the shore. The brothers James and John started to intervene to protect Jesus, but He waved them off and allowed this odd man to grovel before Him. The man continued his babbling and then became suddenly coherent as he looked to Jesus and cried out, "What have you to do with me, Jesus, Son of the God Most High? I beg you, do not torment me!"

Jesus touched the man on the head and demanded, "Demons who possess this man, leave him at once!" Before us was a great battle. I could feel the presence of evil as it faced off against our Rabbi. The man on his knees before Jesus obviously had been in this state for years, as was evident in the scars on his wrists from the shackles used on demoniacs and the filth that covered his body and matted hair. Jesus, remaining calm, continued to address, not the man, but some thing in the man, "What is your name?"

"Legion" came a scratching voice from deep within the man, "Please, Jesus, Son of the God Most High, do not condemn us into the abyss, but allow us to enter the swine up yonder on the hill."

"Let it be so" Jesus allowed.

The man fell back on the ground into a series of convulsions. Suzanna and I still held each other as gust of spirits, a cloud of black, jolted from the man. The spirits raged and cursed as they rushed from the man to the herd of swine above us on the hill. Suddenly, a great squeal came from the swine-herd and, without warning, they began to stampede full speed down into the sea. They moved as one beast desperate to end life, and had I not pulled Suzanna from their path, I believe they would have taken the two of us with them into the water. Drowning them, the sea steamed as if extinguishing the fire of life.

Quickly, this dramatic story spread throughout the land and we did not get much teaching done before the fearful people asked Jesus to leave. Jesus told us that He came to spread the Word, but if the people refused it He was to walk away and allow them that choice. His Father was not one to force belief, but welcome it. And so, with little done, we loaded up the boat and headed home. I secretly would have liked to stay at least the night on dry land before venturing out to sea again, but I remained silent, trying to follow Suzanna's example, and joined the crew in preparation.

As we were leaving the man whom Jesus had saved ran up to join us and Jesus called him back. "You are to remain at home and declare how much God has done for you."

The man obeyed without question, kissed Jesus' feet, and departed.

Thankfully, our trip back across the sea to Galilee was uneventful and, exhausted, we all fell to a quick sleep back at camp. It was not long before Jesus announced that we were all to leave on our missions and He was staying to spend time alone with His Father. That evening He and I took our usual walk and He reminded me that He would be present with me as I prayed.

I clung to His arm knowing I would miss these walks while we were apart and sensing my sadness, He kissed my forehead and softly cautioned me, "Mary, do not forget to pray and to have faith. It will keep you strong while you are away."

I nodded, not understanding His concern for me; I always pray and after what I had seen in the last few days I would not waiver in faith again, I was sure. I embraced Him and said I would miss Him, but that I knew the physical separation would not break our bond. Little did I know the weakness of my own words.

In the morning, I regretfully said goodbye to Suzanna and Joanna, who went to Caesarea, and began the long journey back to Bethany. Peter and Andrew had found a traveling group of families who let me join them for the journey southward. I had traveled so much during my business years, but now I felt a loneliness along the road; and as I thought of home where I knew my sister was waiting, I felt unsure and afraid. The closer I got, the more I questioned what Jesus had said, that this was a mission for me, that He would be with me.

As we set out, it was not long before the families spilt as the men who traveled much quicker began to be lost over the horizon ahead of us. The first day I enjoyed walking along with the women and children. The children, still fresh and energetic, danced around us in merriment and games. I was sure by the time we stopped to rest in the afternoon, they had actually covered twice as much ground as their mothers with their weaving in and out, running ahead and returning to check in. I reveled in their joy at every new thing they saw along the way. Several older boys, wanting to be old enough to travel with the men, walked in front and tried to keep a steady pace while their siblings raced between them, mocking their feigned leadership. The children kept my mind off my questioning and my worrying about returning home.

As dusk neared we found the camp of men, already set up and waiting for us. A warm welcome was shared as families regrouped and broke off for short reunions. My loneliness returned as I stood alone in the midst of this large family. As the meal was prepared, I tried to step in to help, but the women all had roles and fell right into place. They allowed me to help a bit with the bread and passing meals out, but I felt as though I was in the way. After supper, we settled around the fires, and even though the women included me in conversations, I was very aware of my empty lap as mothers hugged children close kissing foreheads and cleaning faces.

I remembered my dreams of motherhood and a husband to care for me, and I glanced around the circle of women admiring the contentment in their faces. My jealousy was no longer in my heart, but doubt of my present life crept forward. What was I doing? Was I in the right place? I knew I believed in Jesus and His teachings. I knew I was called to follow Him, but what was I doing as a woman among these men of His? Was this the life I was meant to have?

By the time I arrived in Bethany, I had convinced myself that either there would be a group of women waiting eagerly inside Martha's house the moment I arrived or that this was a ruse to patronize my longing to travel with the men. I found the door open and there was Martha cleaning the front room, alone. And so, the latter was my welcome. I came in hoping to find the women, and instead, I found my sister deep in her house cleaning and she was more relieved to find a helper than interested in where I had been and what I had learned. For three days I allowed myself to fall deeper into this self-pity as I went about the tasks my sister laid out for me each morning with a bitterness that stole coldly through my blood.

"Who did I think I was that the Messiah would have any use for me?" I scolded myself as I counted the sheep and opened the gate in the morning.

"Some mission you are on. He was probably ashamed to send you anywhere. After all, He knows what you've done and who you really are." I berated myself on the way to the well in the afternoon, avoiding the other women who would have gone in the morning. I found that I began to avoid people everywhere in my hometown. Did they still look at me as the fool who was a whore to the Romans? I saw in their eyes that they judged me: a divorcee, a used woman, a business shrew. And I began to agree with them. I was all of these things and foolishly, while I traveled with Jesus, I had allowed myself to believe that these were mistakes I had made, not definitions of my self. But, now I donned them once again, forgetting my forgiveness, allowing them to define me.

I slipped so deeply into this darkening of my soul that I questioned whether Jesus, himself, had been laughing at me, and whether I had any worth at all. So, I resigned myself to this depression and decided I would stay with Martha, keep my head down and do the work I was meant to do: clean, cook, tend the sheep. Many a night I went to sleep without my usual prayer and rather than seek Him in the quiet of my meditation, I punished myself for my foolishness and neglected our relationship.

Needless to say, this thrilled Martha. I told her my resolve one morning as I readied the wool for her weaving. She had given up on trying to teach me the loom, for my homemaking talents were still wanting, to say the least. So, it was my job to roll the rough wool against my leg into strands and then to spin them into a thin yarn she could use to create beautiful rugs that her husband sold in the market along with his trading goods. My legs were yet unaccustomed to the chore and the dye irritated my skin where the wool had rubbed it raw. But this morning, as I verbalized my disappointment, I welcomed the pain. I looked up a moment from my work and simply said, "I am staying here with you, Martha."

Standing at the upright loom before her, she turned and smiled, "Mary, you finally are home. I was afraid you would run off quickly again and so, I have not wanted to spark your memory of your travels. A woman is not to be tromping around the region as if she had nothing better to do. I thought you would have learned that through other experiences," her eyes frowned at me in judgment, " but nevertheless, you have learned it now. Welcome home." She stooped over me and embraced me.

"Yes, Martha, I will help you to tend to the

house and I will drop my silly dreams of being a part of the new Kingdom."

"New kingdom? Your friend Jesus is a wise rabbi, but a king? Come now, we have known him since he was a boy, and I agree, he has always been a teacher, but don't you agree that he is a bit odd?"

"Odd?" I almost shouted, for she had not seen what I had seen, experienced the love and power of this man, and she had not even permitted me to speak of Him yet. I was shocked. Couldn't she see? It was not He that was unworthy, it was I who had failed and didn't belong in the Kingdom to come. This is why I was giving up, this was why I was here. But, I couldn't say all of that, for Martha broke in after my initial outburst.

"Oh, Mary, even talk of this disturbs the quiet peace surrounding your chores. Let us leave it and not speak of it again. Tomorrow is wash day and you will enjoy returning to the quiet stream and seeing the women from Bethany again."

The rest of the day we spun in silence, taking occasional breaks for other chores and finally, as dusk arrived, Martha took my hand and led me like a docile sheep from the basket of wool into the house. Obediently, in surrender, I helped her prepare supper for the household.

That night I lay in the dark, feeling its heaviness pressing on me, wanting to cry out to God, but afraid that I had closed that door by my own neglect. I knew I did not want the life I had just committed to. I did not belong here at home with

Martha, but I felt I had no choice; this was all I was capable of. Alone in the night, I tried to accept my station, and finally, in the darkest hours of the night, I desperately fell to my knees and tried the only thing I could: I prayed. However, my meditation was interrupted. Each time I set my mind on Him, a chill pierced me and I felt as if there was a dark shadow creeping up behind me, preventing my prayer. I was out of practice and blamed myself for my failure, even at this. I wept, begging for some companionship, for His hand to come and touch me.

Finally, as I knelt in troubled prayer, I began to recognize the depths I had allowed my soul to descend with my doubts. I closed my eyes and allowed myself to enter the truth of this darkness. As my mind opened to the silence of prayer, a sea surrounded me and for a moment I felt I was home in Magdala. However, as I lay my head back into the cool water I was suddenly gripped with panic. The water was vast and dark and deep. I could not sense what was below me or around me and I wanted to dive in and drowned quickly, end it before some shadowy creature from the bottom could drag me into the abyss. I wanted to know my fate, how ever dismal it was. I looked up into an even darker sky and cried out, "Jesus, come to me!"

At once a hand brushed my hair and with it a calm came over me. The frightening water became a warm bath of the Father's love. Rather than continuing to insist on knowing what lie beneath the water, I felt myself ease into trust again. And with that trust came peace. My heart lifted from the ocean of doubt I had wallowed in as His voice came to me from above. He spoke to every part of my being, "Mary, I am with you always." I fainted into this pool of Love and there I slept until morning.

Chapter 13

I remember the river, my mission...

In the morning I felt my inner connection to Jesus renewed and, with the solitary, thoughtful walk to the town stream, I arrived full of patience for His call. I still did not understand why I had to come home or what I was supposed to do, but I felt comforted as I knew He had not abandoned me in my doubt. A mustard seed, if only I had faith the size of a mustard seed. I couldn't believe I had doubted so again and I now eagerly went about my chores knowing they could be offered up to Him as well as anything else I could do.

The stream first reached me through my ears. The barely audible bubbling of the brook over softened stones and the singing laughter of the women beckoned me with a welcome I almost ran to. I did not comprehend the joy that lifted my heart for these were women who could judge me harshly and I had thus far feared meeting them. However, to my surprise, as I rounded the brush that hid the water, Rebekah, a long time neighbor of ours, embraced me with her round, leathery arms, kissing me to welcome me home. As she did, others followed. It was with her blessing that I was deemed worthy of fellowship by the others. And as I stepped into the refreshing water, I felt a part of my old community: I was just Mary, no business master, no scandalous tarnished whore, just a neighbor, a fellow woman doing my chores with other women. It felt good.

As we started with the first round of clothing, Rebekah began to tell stories to pass the time. She began with the traditional story of a woman of endurance and deep faith, Maccabbee's mother.

"Long, long ago, seven brothers and their mother were arrested by the Hellenistic King Antiochus and ordered to join the pagans in their partaking of swine flesh. They were brought before the King and the eldest son, rugged from his days of oppression, rasped through parched lips, 'what do you intend to ask? For we are ready to die rather than transgress the laws of our ancestors.'

"The king, reacting like one of their enraged pagan gods barked back at him, 'we shall see about that, you who speak of death so easily. I only invite you to dine with my court.'

"He turned to his servants and ordered large pans to be heated over the roaring fire in the center of the court. The Maccabbees had never seen such pans, a whole beast could be cooked at once, head and all, in such pans. They expected a pig to be led in, but no beast was present. The king laughed at their puzzlement as the man-sized pans were brought in and hung over the open flame. Suddenly, a realization hit the Maccabbee family, 'is it us he intends to cook?'

"The eldest bravely stepped in front of the others and stood erect with pride, strengthened by his mother's hand grasped steadily on his shoulder. The horror of what was intended could be imagined, but the full savagery of the king's plan was unthinkable."

Rebekah's audience in the stream had all heard the story, yet, as she spoke, we whispered about the spitting hot pans awaiting the young men and shivered at the horror of it.

She paused to allow our reaction and then began the story again, "The king's guard took the eldest forward, and asked him again, 'Will you not eat the flesh of swine with us?'

"The young man said nothing as he stood before the king. Enraged, the king nodded to his guards who at once grabbed the boy and held him as the king, himself, cut out his tongue. Then the guard standing behind him took the same knife, grabbed the boy's hair and pulled his head back, placed the knife against his forehead, and scalped him. As the boy's face was painted in his own blood, another guard came wielding a large glittering sword and with clean swipes severed his hands. The boy fell to his knees and the guard, as if in a dance, circled the boy and cut off his feet at the ankles."

Several of the women washing in the stream moaned in disgust, beat their chests, and nodded to one another in their sharing sympathy for the witnessing mother as Rebekah's retelling also looked to the mourning mother, "This mother you all mention, though torn apart inside with each abuse on her son, did not cry out, did not beg for her son's life, but stood in faith as her son had done and flinched not. And the torture continued. For as the eldest crumbled helplessly to the ground, the king, whose blood-thirst was not yet appeased, had the boy thrown onto the frying pan.

"His brothers choked on the smoke of the burning flesh and boiling blood curdling in their nostrils..." At this point a few women close to Rebekah splashed her with water to get her to stop her horrible description. She only rebuked them, saying, "We must live our history with all senses, remembering it by bringing it back in full reality to us. There is no softening of tales among women; we must relive it all together. So, as I was saying, while the brothers choked on the spreading smoke of the burning flesh and boiling blood curdling in their nostrils, their mother stood strong and encouraged her sons saying, 'The Lord God is with us and feels compassion for us as Moses sang about when he said 'And He will have compassion on his servants'."

Rebekah's voice sang out the next five sons' deaths with the same vivid description and passion as she did the first. We washed in the running water and listened, our bodies methodically working at the stones, but our souls lifting to heaven united with the remembered faith of the Maccabbees.

As we finished our laundry, she came to the youngest son, a child martyred with the same courage shown by his older brothers, "The king paused in his cruelty and offered the youngest boy riches and privilege if he abandoned the way of his ancestors. He offered the mother a chance to convince her only remaining son to save his life and give in to the king. The mother nodded to the king and began to plead with her son. However, she spoke in their native tongue so only the child would understand her. While the court arrogantly assumed she was pleading with him to save his life, in reality, what she said to her last living child was this, 'My son, pity me. I carried you, I bore you, I've reared you thus far, but you are not mine. God made you from things that did not exist before. Do not fear this butcher, but prove worthy of your brothers. Accept death, so that in God's mercy, you will be returned to me with your brothers one day.'

"And the boy, a child tender in youth but unyielding in spirit, challenged the king, 'what are you waiting for? I, like my brothers, forfeit body and life for the laws of our ancestors. I appeal to God's mercy for our nation and by trials and plagues to make you confess that He alone is God, and through me and my brothers to bring an end to His wrath that justly falls on our nation'".

As we women at the wash listened, tears mingled with our river water as we wept in cathartic community. Finally, with relief, we heard the mother's death, reprieve after having witnessed such a slaughter of her household.

I sighed, exhausted: not from labor, but from thousands of years of oppression, from the tested strength the Jewish people have displayed over and over, and from my own shallow faith that had seen no purpose in my coming home to the women of my community. As I said my goodbyes and walked back to Martha's home I realized that this was the group of women I was to find here. I knew nothing more about what I was to do, but I knew that today I had been shown the ministry Jesus had intended for me.

The next week went quickly with me going about my chores with dutiful joy. Recalling the community at the river lightened my spirit and I praised my wise teacher: I needed this. In my quiet meditation while kneading bread for the household, I reflected on what I had desired verses what I had received. My mind had desired to be the head of a great crowd, moving them with wise words, leading them as Jesus does. But a cold, arrogant feeling swept over me as I now recalled this imagined scene. What I had received in coming home was very different: The actualization of my calling was an intimate sharing of hearts found only among that close community of women. I finally got it. I needed to return home, to join a small community to find my mustard seed of faith. God was here, inside my heart, not in grand booming measures, but in a tender loving whisper. Here it was again, that presence of God I sought: Shechina. And again, it came in soft whispers.

When wash day arrived my heart leapt in anticipation of seeing my friends again and sharing the blessings of our closeness. I tried to guess what story would be shared today as I carried my wash, the load seemingly much lighter than the week before; Maybe it would be devious Delilah or jealous Rachel or brave Esther. In my mind, I ran through many of the wonderful women of our tradition, remembering each story with a pride in my heritage. As I found my spot and began to set up my wash, a young bride named Anna, turned to me and called out, "Mary, are you not the one they've talked about?" Before she could finish her thought my face flushed ready for her to recall my sins, but her sentence did not end with gossip, instead, she asked, "Are you the one who traveled with the great Rabbi?"

"Yes, I have traveled with Jesus," I replied as I let out a long breath of relief.

"Tell us. Tell us what it is like to walk with Him," her enthusiasm danced out of her as the others joined in, all wanting to hear about Jesus.

"Well, I don't know where to begin, " I stuttered, for I hadn't expected to speak so soon.

As I mused over the many wonders I had seen and stories I had heard, a bitter comment from a harsh, frail, old woman cut the air, "I hear He is bringing a Kingdom for the Jews. Is Kingdom building not the job of men? What care could this teacher possibly have for the plight of women? We bow to whatever king our men bow to."

Her challenge inadvertently pointed me in the direction of a story. Leah, the bitter old woman, brought to mind as if in contrasting reflection, a woman who showed the power of her faith in Jesus; the woman with the hemorrhages. And so, in answer to her, I began, "Well, let me tell you of a woman whose faith has a lot to do with His Kingdom. It was just before He sent us on our mission," I smiled as my mission unfolded before me. I was indeed sharing His teachings with a crowd, a very important crowd: women. "We had arrived back in Capernaum when we were met by a large crowd. As you have no doubt heard, His reputation as a healer is growing and He is often being called on to visit the sick. On that day, Janius, leader of the Synagogue in the North, was pleading with Jesus to come and cure his daughter who had grown quite ill. Jesus, of course, agreed to go and headed straight to the house, crowds following.

"There were times when the crowds pressed us so against one another that I lost my breath. Peter, Andrew, and John, apostles who are quite protective of our Teacher, tended to surround Him for fear He himself would be trampled by the swarms. He usually rebukes them as He is completely centered and relaxed amidst any number or class of people. On this day the crowd was swelling to the very walls of the narrow streets. As we came to an open courtyard, however, Jesus stopped and turned to us, asking 'Who touched me?'

"Peter quickly jumped in saying, 'Master, the crowd surrounds you, many have probably touched you'. You could feel his fear of failure as he interpreted the touch as a violation that he and his brother had failed to stop.

"'No Peter,' Jesus said, with his hand on Peter's shoulder, assuring him, 'Someone touched me with faith, for I felt power go out from me.'

"The crowd looked around for the offender and finally a woman came forth shakingly confessing. She fell down before Him, weeping her story, ' For 12 years,' she wailed, 'I have bled. Rabbis, physicians, they have all tried to help me, draining me of every possession I have. An unclean woman, I have wondered the streets begging. My neighbors toss me food as if I were an animal; they are afraid to be defiled by my touch. I live alone among the masses: invisible.'"

I paused as my audience sighed with sympathy for the woman. I nodded along with them and continued, "And she said as she looked up at Jesus from her place at His feet, 'But I knew if I could but touch the hem of your cloak, that I would be healed, and I am. At once I was cleansed, my pain flew from me as if exorcised and I stand here before you a clean woman.'

"The crowd turned to Jesus as she silenced and bowed her head. Peter looked defiantly at her, arms crossed, ready to watch his master wreak His wrath upon this woman who had defiled Him. We all expected it, a rebuke, a punishment, for she had broken the Law. But He is never what we expect. Did it matter that she had not asked in a formal way for healing? Did it matter that she, an outcast, dared join a crowd, spreading her defilement? Did it matter that she risked defiling the Rabbi himself?"

I let the questions hang in the air as the women grappled with the laws of cleanliness verses their clear pity for this woman.

"No" I dropped into their musing, "Jesus cared only for the woman and her affliction. He took her trembling hands in His, steadied her and looked her right in the eye and said to her, 'Daughter, your faith has made you whole; go in peace.'"

With that, the end of my story, the women around me in the river cheered and heralded Jesus as the wisest of teachers as well as an incredible healer.

However, Leah was not so easily impressed. The old woman shifted her stance, staring at her wash and muttered, "I don't know about His breaking the Laws. What sort of Kingdom will this leader bring us if He, Himself, can break the

Laws of Moses for any individual he wishes? That would be chaos!"

The others ignored her and began chattering about the wisdom of His love and how He was not like the Pharisees who blanketed themselves in cumbersome rules. Anna, the young girl who had prompted my telling jumped in with, "And He called her 'daughter'. A family. That's what he has brought us, a family." She said this not directly to answer Leah's retort, but we all heard the connection.

"Why, he reasons like a woman," Rebekah chimed in with her compliment. "If only all men were so wise as to weigh the person before the Law, we might not ever have chaos, now would we?" She then directly addressed Leah's bitterness, "It is a wise leader who sees the person before Him and recognizes that the rules exist for us, not us for the rules. Did not even King David break the law when he brought his men to eat the sacred Bread of the Presence so they would not starve?"

Leah just scoffed at the comparison of the two. However, I pointed out that Jesus was of the line of David since Joseph, Mary's husband, is a direct descendant. With that we left Leah to her fussing and went back to celebrating the story of the woman's healing.

Later that evening, as I prayed about Leah, I thought of the parable of the sower and I saw the weeds pulling her from hearing the Truth of Jesus. I prayed that His hand would come to gather her in as it had gathered me.

Chapter 14

I remember His visit...

I enjoyed the next couple of months with my community. We now met at the well each morning for a short prayer together as we got the day's water, and we continued to take turns telling stories of our tradition and parables of Jesus on wash day. Anna, the youngest of our group, had memorized many of the parables I told and enjoyed retelling them herself when it was her turn. More incredibly, my sister, Martha, had even begun to show interest in my stories and she often joined us at the river.

Slowly, she began to question me about my experiences as she heard of my teaching from the other women. Though she still feared it would send me away from home again, she was coming around to at least being curious about what I had learned. One night, at supper, Martha said to Ronen, "Have you heard of the stories my sister has been telling around town?"

"Yes, the men say their wives come home with stories of healings and miracles, and they keep their children around the fire eagerly telling parables. What is it Mary," he turned to address me, "that you hope to achieve here?"

Stunned by his accusation of some grand plan, I stuttered in reply, "Achieve? I have no plan, Ronen. Jesus is the one who knows the ultimate goal. I only have my work to share the good news. It is not for me to know beyond that."

"Well, it is causing quite a stir, and yet, I have not heard anything from you two. Why is it that you do not share this 'good news' at home?" he asked lightening his tone. He too was at least curious about Jesus.

"I forbade her upon her return to speak of her travels, my husband," Martha answered for me, "but I do wish, if Ronen approves, that you tell us a bit of what you have been through. I feel a bit foolish when I meet the women you speak with and do not know what they refer to."

"Yes," Ronen piped in, "We do need to be let in on this. Perhaps a story or two at dinner each night, just so we know what our neighbors speak of, you understand."

"Of course," I replied, smiling inside, for I thought of dear Joanna's lesson: it did not matter why one comes to Jesus, only that we all seek Him out in our own way, "just so you know what the neighbors speak of, sure, of course."

That night I began to share at home. Because Ronen had always shown such hospitality to my family and myself, and because he had always opened his home to me without question after each of my returns from the world, I began with the story of the Prodigal Son, a favorite of mine.

"Jesus tells us of renewal and forgiveness in the story of the man with two sons. It goes like this, 'A wealthy man, a trader I am sure, had two sons. The youngest son demanded one day that he receive his inheritance at once rather than wait until the old man's passing. The old man, loving his son, agreed and split his wealth equally between his children.

"The eldest continued his work at home, not changing a thing with all the new wealth he received. However, the younger son, more rash and adventurous," I smiled at Martha as we both clearly saw the reflection of ourselves in the story, "took off to see the world and enjoy the fortune. He sought out far off places and there he spent his money on drink, women, and games. However, as his money depleted, so did his luck. For not long after he had spent his last coin, a famine swept over the region where he now lived. Starving and out of money, the young man sought work feeding pigs. A lowly job with little pay and no comfort. Finally, he realized that he could go home and beg his father for a job, for surely his father would pay him better, and the servants he grew up with had comfortable quarters and fine meals every day.

"With that he humbly headed home and planned his apology as he walked. ' I will fall to my father's feet and beg for mercy. I will say to him, Father I have sinned against both you and heaven and I am no longer worthy of the title 'son'. Please take me in as a hired hand. Allow me to beg at your door-step'.

"This was his plan. However, as he approached his childhood home, his father saw him coming and ran out to meet him. He embraced his lost son and called for a great party to be held in his honor. The son tried to get out the apology that he had rehearsed along the journey, but his father would have none of it. Instead, he covered him in new robes, offered him fine wine, and prepared a great feast.

"The faithful older brother, you can imagine, was not at all pleased with the reception this brat received and he complained to his father, 'Father, I have been here working for you all these years. I have stayed here, obeyed every command, and yet, I have never had a feast with my friends of even the smallest of your goats. Yet, this son of yours who has been whoring and gambling away your fortune, he is welcomed like a king!'

"The father, taking the eldest son's hand, said to him, 'My son, you are my heart. Everything I have is yours, but it is right to celebrate with your brother. For he was dead to us and here he returns, he was lost and is now found. Rejoice with me.'

"This is where Jesus ended his story, but when I meditate on it, I find myself imagining further. I am sure, or rather, hopeful that the brother returned to the feast, realizing his jealous folly, and embracing his brother with love, welcoming him home."

My story ended as Martha cleared away the dishes from our evening meal. She smiled and turned to me, "Yes, I am sure he embraced his wandering brother and welcomed him home."

Ronen stood silently and retired to the more comfortable cushions around the fire. As he stared into the flames, I followed him over to the fire and sat, respecting his silence, waiting for his response. As Martha returned to us, he said, "This Jesus is a wise teacher. I see the wisdom in what your friend preaches. Perhaps we will be fortunate enough to welcome Him into our home one day."

That was all he said, but that did not surprise me. Ronen was a man of few words, but his actions and his gentle ways showed his good heart. It was not long before his hope of welcoming Jesus was realized, for a few weeks later I received word that my Lord was coming to visit.

I was returning home with water one morning when young Anna ran up to me.

"Mary, they've come," she stammered between long breaths.

"Who? Who has come?" I asked.

"The Rabbi and His disciples," she glowed with excitement.

By the time we reached the top of the last hill before Martha's house I could see the crowd gathering in the vast pastures that surrounded the small dwelling. Even from this distance I could see my sister trying her best to welcome each guest, many from our own town, and assure that every person was comfortable and had whatever they needed. It is a beautiful sight to see a natural hostess in her element and I paused to admire Martha's warmth turning a crowd into a family. As we neared, she stepped out delegating to both Anna and myself.

"Mary," she said, "Go in and greet your friends, and be sure they have accommodations for the night." I started heading to the house, when she grabbed my arm and added, "If they do not, we can house 3 or 4 and you can send Anna here into town to assure rooms at the inn." I nodded, laughing at her urgency over matters I had routinely taken care of while I traveled.

My excitement grew as I ran to the house and burst through the door. There I found Jesus with His arms open wide as if He were aware of my approach. As we embraced, a light shot through my being and I lingered there, taking in the feel of His touch, the smell of His body, the sound of His steady breath. He pulled me back, kissed me, and turned to greet Anna, who shyly waited just behind me.

Peter popped up with a warm arm around my shoulders whispering in my ear, "Mary, I've got so much to tell you!" I smiled and embraced my friend, eager to again share his enthusiasm. I had missed my friends and tears of joy filled my eyes at this unexpected reunion.

Remembering Martha's order, I quizzed Peter about their accommodations and he assured me they were fine camping just outside of town. However, that was too far away for me and so I turned back to Jesus and pleaded with Him that He and Peter stay with us. Peter joined in, and with a little prodding, He relented agreeing that a good night's sleep would not hurt Him.

With our welcomes said, Jesus went out to greet the crowds and share His teachings with them. I sought out Ronen and made sure he had a seat with Anna, Peter, and myself right at the feet of Jesus to devour every drop of His wisdom. James, the tender and eager student, requested, "Lord, teach us to pray, as John taught his disciples."

Jesus looked to the crowd and said to them, "When you pray, say this:

Father, hallowed be your name.
Your kingdom come.
Give us each day our daily bread
And forgive us our sins,
For we ourselves forgive
Everyone indebted to us.
And do not bring us to the time of trial.
Amen"

We all echoed with a definitive "AMEN". I looked around for my sister, wanting to share this moment with her, but all the while Jesus was teaching, Martha continued her hostessing. Catching her eye, I called her over. However, she strode right past me, and she approached Jesus complaining, "Lord, do you not care that my sister has left me to do all the work myself? Tell her to help me." I was surprised at her complaint, and I flushed under her criticism.

Jesus answered her, "Martha, Martha," taking the basket of bread from her hand and setting it on he ground, "you are worried and distracted by many things." She nodded at His understanding of her stress and was calmed by His touch. He turned her around to us saying, "There is only one thing. Mary has chosen the better part, which will not be taken from her. These things can wait. You will not always have me. Sit." I expected a rebuttal from my sister, but instead, Martha took a deep breath, nodded to Jesus, and settled on the ground with us.

I took her hand and whispered, "Thank you for all you have done to welcome my friends." She smiled and squeezed my hand, grateful for my appreciation, as Jesus continued to talk about prayer. She knew I was not the hostess she was and in that smile said that she accepted me.

Jesus, speaking to the demands of a hostess, told us all this story: "Suppose one of you has a friend, and you go to him at midnight and say to him, 'Friend, lend me three loaves of bread; for a friend of mine has arrived, and I have nothing to set before him.' And he answers from within, 'Do not bother me; the door has already been locked, and my children are with me in bed; I cannot get up and give you anything.' I tell you, if he continues to knock, even though he will not get up and give him anything because he is a friend, at least because of his persistence he will get up and give him whatever he needs.

"So I say to you, ask, and it will be given you; search, and you will find; knock, and the door will be opened for you. For everyone who asks receives, and everyone who searches finds, and for everyone who knocks, the door will be opened. Is there anyone among you who, if your child asks for a fish, will give a snake instead of a fish? Or if the child asks for an egg, will give a scorpion? If you then, you who are evil, know how to give good gifts to your children, how much more will the heavenly Father give the Holy Spirit to those who ask him!"

As Jesus paused and allowed us to take in what he was teaching, I thought of how I had asked for a mission like all the other missions, and in His wisdom, He had given me a mission that was so much more valuable for me. I did not even know what I was asking for, but the Father and this, His Son, knew what I needed and gave me more than I ever could have imagined or asked for. The crowd began to discuss the teaching and I went to Jesus and said, "Thank you for knowing what I asked for, even when I was not aware of what I wanted."

"Your time here then has been what you needed?" He asked.

"Oh, Teacher, it has been more than I could have ever put into words to ask. The community of women has fed my spirit. Together we have explored the traditions of our people and opened each other to your teachings. I have been welcomed back into the world of women, which I discarded years ago after my failure at motherhood and my descent into sin. I feel myself growing each day."

"Yes, once the Father had forgiven and healed you, you needed to face home, forgive yourself, and accept the forgiveness of your family here. You are ready to rejoin us; however, your family will need you soon, and so we will be saying a farewell once again." Noting my disappointed look, He took my hand and added, "a short one this time. We will return for you soon."

We returned to the group in silence and after he gave a closing blessing to the crowd, they dispersed and we went inside to sit by the hearth. Soon everyone headed for bed except Peter and myself. He had nudged me again on the way in and asked me to stay up with him by the fire to talk. I sat at the fire as he rushed over to speak to Jesus for a moment before He left the front room. After a short, quiet conversation, Jesus looked over from Peter to me, smiled and nodded His head as He strolled off to bed. Peter returned and said to me, "Do you know who Jesus is?"

I was puzzled and sat dumb waiting for him to answer his own question.

"I am to tell no one about this but you. And so you must not share it either until the time comes." I nodded silently moving in closer to hear every word and wondering what Peter meant by “the time”. What time?

He did not answer that question, but continued to share an incredible witness with me. “One evening Jesus invited myself, James, and John up to the mountain to join Him for his evening prayers. It began like any other night. He went ahead as we stayed a bit down the slope. We all knelt to pray and suddenly I was blinded by a brightness that shone from Jesus.” At this point, Peter’s enthusiasm pushed him from his chair and he stood before me with the shadows from the fire playing on the wall opposite him as his arms whirled before him.

“His cloak was white as the morning sun and a radiance warmed my face as I looked on Him. As my eyes adjusted I saw two men standing with Him. And, now, you are not going to believe this; we didn’t until we confirmed it with one another, but the men were Moses and Elijah in all their heavenly glory! We approached hesitantly and heard them talking about Jesus’ triumphant departure from Jerusalem that is fast approaching.”

“Departure?” I interrupted, “Where is He going? Are we going with Him?”

“That part is not clear to us, even today. Anyway, standing there, I blurted out before thinking, ‘Master, it is good for us to be here; let us make three dwellings - one for you, one for Moses, and one for Elijah’. Can you believe what a fool I am? What sort of dwelling could I offer them?”

I smiled as I shared his embarrassment, covering

my mouth to hide any trace of the giggle that grew in my throat. He continued, "Thankfully, I was interrupted before my foolishness was laughed at. We were suddenly enveloped by a great cloud! It was as if the whale of Jonah came from the sky and swallowed us in his great jaws. Thick fog separated me from my companions and I trembled trying to stare into the thick dark sea around us." Peter's arms continued to swirl, now in the fashion of swimming through the air before him as he relayed this vision to me. His shadow on the wall behind him darkened into the shape of a whale as he continued, "And from every part of the cloud I heard a voice. I don't know how to explain the voice...it was..."

"I know," I said looking down at the fire, "I have heard it."

He looked at me oddly, and I nodded for him to continue his witness. He continued, "The voice knocked us to the ground as it boomed, 'This is my Son, my Chosen. Listen to Him!'"

He leaned back against the wall and crossed his arms, watching me, waiting for me to take it all in. I smiled and said, "So, it is true? He is, then? The Messiah? The Son of God?"

"Yes," Peter confirmed.

We sat, connected by our joint realization of what we were a part of, not knowing what to say for a long time. Finally, Peter inquired about my claim to have heard the voice, and I told him about the baptism with John and what I had witnessed. It felt good to finally open up completely sharing all the stirrings of my heart about who Jesus was and my conviction to help Him bring about the Kingdom He spoke of. We still had little knowledge of the true meaning of all that was going on, and we knew that; but a clarity came as we shared our faith and we welcomed the deeper understanding.

As we stood, exhausted from our sharing, and embraced to head off for sleep, I noticed another shadow on the wall across the room from where we stood. I turned to see its source and found Jesus standing in the corner of the room. Startled, I jumped back and Peter spun around to also find our Lord. He smiled at us and whispered, "Whenever two or more of you are gathered in my name, there I too will be." We went to Him and again I found myself lost in Him embrace. He kissed each of us and sent us off to sleep while He lingered near the fire, alone.

Chapter 15

I remember my brother's healing...

Not long after the group left I found that my family did, indeed, need me. My brother, Lazarus, sent word from Magdala that his family had grown ill and he needed our help. A flash of the young girl from the Jerusalem Market a year ago came into my mind. The plague up there had wiped out her family; I wondered how she had fared. Immediately, I offered to travel north and find out what was going on. Ronen arranged for me to travel with a group of traders from his business. And so, I found myself on the road again.

The luxury of their accommodations reminded me of the travels I had done with my father for business. Each night, even when we camped, we slept on soft cushions of wool and were fed fine meals of fruit and meat. At first, I was leery of being in among men on my own. It was not like traveling with Jesus and His followers. These men were lustful, worldly men, and I feared their glances. The only security I had was the word of Ronen who now seemed far away as we ventured north along the Jordan. I stayed nearest the eldest member whom they all seemed to respect and in whose company I felt a kind of fatherly protection. At night I went to my tent early and fell into long meditative prayers until I heard the last of their voices fade from the center fire replaced by loud, manly snoring.

As the days continued, the men began to speak to me, and in that familiarity I, at last, found security. By the fifth day of travel, I had been welcomed in as a companion and now there would be no threat to me; I was part of the group. That night, I joined them around the fire as they told stories of conquest and bravery, and I was happy to be invited to listen.

The most lively story was told by the elder I continued to cling to, Zachariah, whose long beard and wise eyes reminded me of my father. Zachariah told the story of David's conquest over Goliath, the Giant. He marched around the fire as he told of the threat to the Israelites and the flicker of the flames gave exaggerated drama to his every move. The energy within the group grew with each detail, and I found myself caught up in the camaraderie as I joined the men in their victorious battle cry as David's stone found its mark. Feeling like victors and ready to brave any danger the night might bring, the men joined Zachariah in his march around the fire, proud to be David's people.

I felt like a child again, keeping company with my father's men. I had not heard a story told with such fire since my father had passed away. I closed my eyes and imagined him here with us, joining us in our triumph over the invading tribe of Goliath's people. Those were the grand days of the Israelites. David, our proud and powerful king of our own land, our own nation. Would we be there again, I wondered. I thought of Jesus' kingdom. It could be no less. He was, after all, of David's line, therefore, a king Himself. I left the men to their celebration as I wondered to my tent musing about the Kingdom to come and how these men might one day be instrumental in helping Jesus to bring it about.

As I drifted off to sleep I realized how long it had been since I had taken the time to enjoy the culture of men outside of what I thought I could gain from them; and it was quite an experience to be there with them as a group and not be conspiring in my mind for one of their purses or pleasures. They were a jovial troop who brought wine to the fire and traveled at a leisurely pace. I enjoyed them greatly and appreciated their taking me on as a fellow traveler.

On the last night of our journey, a younger man filled with the bile of hatred I had seen in Judas, reminded us of the "giant" we faced today: The Romans. With their support of King Herod, he had committed ghastly violence upon his own people to obtain power. This younger man told the story of Arbel, a village west of the Sea of Galilee that is framed by honeycomb-like cliffs of caves.

He began, "Let us remember the battles of our fathers, for there is a giant we face today: Rome, who shows no mercy and who supports men who are not filled with the Spirit. Remember Arbel."

The men around the fire, lacking the enthusiasm of the night before, bowed their heads and nodded. It was a sad story and was often used to stir the crowds who occasionally dared to rise up against the Emperor.

The young traveler continued, "There, at Arbel, when Herod's rival Antigonus dared to meet him in battle, Herod slew many Jews to gain power. My grandfather was there and told me as a young man of the cries of the women as they were dragged from their caves. For the wise Antigonus had hid his fellow rebels and their wives and children in the wall of cliffs, thinking they were safe. However, crafty Herod lowered men down in baskets from atop the cliffs. As his warriors hung safely out of the reach of the rebels, they threw grappling hooks in to snag the helpless women and children and drag them to the mouth of the cave. As they laughed at the torture they caused, these barbarians shook their victims off the massive hooks to drop them to their deaths far below. The families, if not killed by the hook itself, perished as they plunged to the shadowy valley of death."

Together my companions beat their chests and nodded in grief, for many of them had also been at the battle. The cries at Arbel, I have heard, seemed unending as the dead died slowly and painfully. The echo off the steep cliffs carried the sorrow out over the Sea of Galilee below as Herod watched his bloody siege. As the young man finished his telling, the tension of an oppressed people dampened the warmth of the fire and we silently drifted to our tents. As I lay on my bedroll, the fears Judas had awakened in my heart of a coming battle, were renewed, and I realized a hatred of the Romans lay just beneath the surface in us all.

By the time we reached Magdala, however, my worries turned to my brother and his family and I rushed down the familiar streets to the small dwelling they lived in not far from the center market. I slowed my run as the door came into view. It was closed and dressed for mourning. I feared what I would find, and my fears were realized as a pale and sallow Lazarus greeted me as best he could. His family was gone, and by the looks of it, he was not far behind them. I told him we needed to get him down to Martha soon, for she was the nurturing one, and it panicked me a bit to think of caring for my sick brother alone. I had volunteered to travel up here, thinking I was the most seasoned traveler, but I had forgotten to consider what might await me upon my arrival.

As we sat in his main room, Lazarus told me of the sickness. It came with a great fever and settled in one's body as if taking up residence. "My wife," he explained, "I had known her all my life, and yet, in her last week, I knew her not. The incomprehensible rambling, the screams in the middle of the night, it is as if she was taken from me long before her body cooled in death."

I had little to offer but condolences and hope for his own recovery. I left him soon after I arrived to seek out my traveling companions to find us a safe return passage home to Martha. I knew she would know much more than I about how to help our brother. When I found the men I had traveled with, they connected me to a small band headed to Jerusalem in two days who were willing to take on the two of us. That is, if my brother was healthy. I knew we would not be allowed to travel with a group the way he was for fear of exposure, and I had no idea what I was going to do to make him healthy in such a short time. But I had to try. I cleaned and aired the house, releasing the sickness that hung heavy in every room. I refreshed his water and put him to bed. The best of my nursing and my endless prayers brought him to a reasonable traveling health just in time for us to leave with the band for the south. I sent word ahead to Martha to have her husband meet us at the crossroad that led west toward Jerusalem for the last leg of the journey and explained his symptoms so she could prepare for Lazarus' care. Finally, I procured a mule and cart so that Lazarus could ride as much of the journey as possible without making it obvious that he was ill.

The trip homeward was not nearly as enjoyable as my trip here. I did not spend my evenings with the group, but back at our cart cooling Lazarus with a wet cloth, telling him the stories of Jesus and reciting prayers with him until he fell into a restless slumber. When we arrived home, Martha was waiting with open door and open arms. She had set up a bed for Lazarus in the back room where it was most cool, and we carried him in right away. Then she and I sat down to discuss his care.

"He does not look well." Martha began.

"No, and he tells me the stages his family went through with this fever as if marking his own impending death."

"I will do my best, and the herbs should cool him. I wonder, should we call for a Rabbi?"

"No," I surprised myself that I had not thought of this before, "We should call for THE Rabbi!"

Knowing I meant Jesus, Martha said, discouraged, "Yes, but where do we find Him?"

"I will put word out around town. It is not rare to hear of where He is preaching and where He is headed. Besides, He knows we need Him before we ask. Let us send word, for He shall come and save our brother," I stated with complete confidence.

With that agreed we sent a letter to Him, saying, "Lord, he whom you love is ill." and we waited.

A week we waited. He did not come.

Finally, after ten long days of suffering, Lazarus gave into his fever and died early one morning. I could not believe Jesus had forsaken us, and in anguish over my brother's death and anger at his being forgotten by the Lord, I tore my cloak. Where was He? I feared our message did not get through; I feared He was somehow unable to reach us; I feared He had forgotten about us. And so, with heavy hearts we planned the funeral. We prepared the house for mourning and set out to bury our brother in a tomb just outside of town.

I numbly recited the Psalm in our funeral procession, "You who live in the shelter of the Most High, who abide in the shadow of the Almighty, will say to the Lord, 'My refuge and my fortress; my God, in whom I trust.'"

My tears flowed as I questioned my trust in Jesus, why did He not come? I could hardly continue with the recitation, but for my brother's sake, forced myself to recount the seven stages of life as we made our stops along the way to his tomb. At our last stop I cried to the skies the final verse, wanting the Father to hear my every word, "When they call to me, I will answer them; I will be with them in trouble, I will rescue them and honor them. With long life I will satisfy them and show them my salvation."

We called! Where is our answer? I wanted to add, but instead, I fell to the ground with Martha clinging to my arm, sharing my distress. She lifted me back to my feet and together we found the strength to complete the funeral.

Slowly, we returned home, lit the Shiva candle, removed our sandals, and welcomed our community as they came to console us. It cheered me a bit to share stories of Lazarus, the memories of his good life; but I could not shake the anger I felt toward God and toward Jesus. Several days later, one of our neighbors who had been with Jesus, said he heard that He was on His way to us. Too late, I thought and I could not move, but Martha jumped up in anticipation.

"I will go meet Jesus", she proclaimed as she readied herself and headed out the door. We were not to travel for three more days yet, and her husband reminded her of her Shiva duty to remain in the home, but I just watched her, hopelessly. I don't know what she hoped to achieve, for he could cure the ill, but Lazarus had been gone for three days now. I could see nothing but comfort available to us and I was sure I was inconsolable. And so I waited at the house for Him. Martha later told me about their encounter.

She said she had seen Jesus and the crowd following him from a distance and ran to Him falling against His chest with her fists, saying, "Lord, if you had been here, my brother would not have died. But even now I know that God will give you whatever you ask of Him."

Jesus grabbed her hands, held her back looking into her eyes and replied, "Martha, your brother will rise again."

"Yes, I know he will rise again on the last day in the resurrection." She agreed taking this as consolation.

But then He said something that evidently surprised her, for she shook even when she told me about it later that night. He declared, "I am the resurrection and the life. Those who believe in me, even though they die, will live, and everyone who lives and believes in me will never die. Do you believe this?"

She had answered, "Yes, Lord, I have come to believe that you are the Messiah, the Son of God, the One coming into the world." I was astounded when she told me this. Martha had begun to study with me the teachings of Jesus, and she even offered to take my place while I traveled to Magdala in sharing the stories with the women during washdays and prayer at the well each morning, but I had not yet asked her to confirm her faith. Her conversion to full belief had happened while I was gone she told me and she said, "It is in the sharing of faith that one's own grows. While I told the stories of the wonders you had witnessed, I found myself experiencing them myself in my heart and mind. I practiced each night hearing your tellings with my head, my heart, and my soul as you taught me, and I have come to believe as you believe."

When she returned from her meeting Him and professing her faith, she had come to the house ahead of Him to call me out. She had said to me,

"The Teacher is here and is calling for you." I had planned on being stubborn, on staying set in my anger, but at the sound of His request I leapt out of the house and ran to meet Him. I ran to the center of town, near the well with the other mourners following me and found Him among his disciples.

I fell to Jesus' feet and cried, "Lord, if you had been here, my brother would not have died."

He joined me in my sorrow and began to weep, asking, "Where have you laid him?"

I could not speak through my tears, so as He helped me to my feet, I pointed Him in the direction of the tomb. The crowd around us began to grumble, some noting the great love Jesus had had for Lazarus which poured out in His tears, others scolding Him for not being here earlier to save him. We walked again on the path of the funeral procession to the tomb and Jesus called for the stone to be removed.

Martha cautioned Him, saying, "Lord, already there is a stench because he has been in there for days."

Unmoved in His resolve, He reminded her, "Did I not tell you that if you believed, you would see the glory of God?"

Obediently, several of his disciples rolled the enormous boulder from the mouth of the cave. We all stepped back from the thick decaying air that escaped. Jesus, who was not moved by the smell, looked upward and with open hands reaching to heaven prayed, "Father, I thank you for having heard me. I know that you always hear me, but I have said this for the sake of the crowd standing here, so that they may believe that you sent me." Then looking into the dark cave He commanded, "Lazarus, come out!"

We stood, silent, waiting. Even those who had grumbled earlier said nothing. And suddenly, out of the darkness appeared my brother, alive! For a moment we stood in silent awe staring at the linen-bound corpse standing before us. Then, as we realized it was indeed our own brother, Martha and I rushed forward and began unwrapping the burial cloths. Lazarus, himself, reached up to uncover his own face blinking at the brightness of the sun. Jesus smiled and said, "Yes, unbind him and let him go."

The next several days were like celebrating a birth. Neighbors came to see and talk with Lazarus, bringing gifts of wine and sweetmeats. Finally, after we were able to wrap our minds around the truth that our hearts had welcomed instantly, that Lazarus had been dead and now sat before us alive, we began to grapple with the question that hung in the room around us all, "What was it like? Olam Ha-Ba. Does it exist?"

Of course, it was Peter, always bold with his questions, who voiced what we all wondered as he approached Lazarus one morning asking, "Tell us Lazarus, what is death?"

Lazarus began slowly, searching for words, "It was, well, it was similar to sleep. However, not in the sleep we experience here. You see, I was not alone in my slumber. My spirit slept not in the small, dark cavern of my body, but within...beside, no, in communion with my loved ones and others who were there. Shadows of life, whispers of love embraced me in welcome as I lay, seemingly waiting for something. And not only their presence, but yours as well surrounded me. I was warmed by your prayers for my soul." He squeezed my hand and kissed it, smiling into my eyes and I knew he had heard my tireless lamenting.

He continued, again struggling to put it into words for us, "There are sensations I can not feed to your senses. There is a love I cannot capture in these small nets called words no matter how many of them I string together. And yet, what I can tell you is this: There is much excitement among the souls of the prophets and our people. Their sleep is to be awakened. Anticipation for the Messiah, the First Risen, is growing, for He must be very near. And His time is coming."

Gasps came from several people in the room and whispers began to puzzle over these words. Peter threw a look to me just as I had turned to look at him. We nodded and in unison declared, "Indeed, He is quite near!"

As the speculations grew, I noticed Jesus stepping out, separating Himself from the crowd, and I excused myself to follow Him. I found Him sitting on Martha's low stone wall, and as I approached Him, I laid my hand on His shoulder to offer comfort and thanks for His love of my brother.

"Mary," He uttered quietly as He turned to me, "my heart. Together we will see the Kingdom."

"Israel? A kingdom. Oh, I dream of such and you know we are ready to go into battle with you."

"My dear Mary," He corrected me, "Do not listen to the aggressive rambling of the men who speak of this world. I speak of the Kingdom of Heaven, and I see that it is time now to clarify that to you, my disciples. This will be *my* battle, for all." He took my hand in both of His and I knew enough to hold my tongue though I stood bewildered and full of questions. However, in my mind, I pictured Him as his ancestor David facing the Giant of Rome all alone.

I looked to the horizon and sat silently beside Jesus watching the sun set with my head resting on His shoulder and my hand warmed in His. I could feel Him take in a deep breath as He pondered things I could not yet understand. And yet, without knowing what His mind struggled with, I felt I shared with Him this moment and this struggle. We sat, holding each other and allowing the evening quiet to enter into our minds. These times of silence were, in fact, when I felt closest to Him. It was as though when we spoke no language at all, the voices of our spirits could converse.

The next morning, Jesus again sat on Martha's low stone wall as He spoke to us about the Kingdom of God. He told us: "Lazarus is right. The Kingdom is at hand."

"What will it be like? This kingdom," asked Judas, still eager to begin his battle.

"Judas, you most of all, listen to what I say. The Kingdom of Heaven may be compared to a king who gave a wedding banquet for his son. He sent his slaves to call those who had been invited to the wedding banquet, but they would not come. Again he sent other slaves, saying, 'Tell those who have been invited: Look, I have prepared my dinner, my oxen and my fat calves have been slaughtered, and everything is ready; come to the wedding banquet.'

"But they made light of it and went away, one to his farm, another to his business, while the rest seized his slaves, mistreated them, and killed them. The king was enraged. He sent his troops, destroyed those murderers, and burned their city. Then he said to his slaves, 'the wedding is ready, but those invited were not worthy. Go therefore into the main streets, and invite everyone you find to the wedding banquet.'

"Those slaves went out into the streets and gathered all whom they found, both good and bad; so the wedding hall was filled with guests. But when the king came in to see the guests, he noticed a man there who was not wearing a wedding robe, and he said to him, 'Friend, how did you get in here without receiving a wedding robe?' And he was speechless. Then the king said to the attendants, 'Bind him hand and foot, and throw him into the outer darkness where there will be weeping and gnashing of teeth.' For many are called, but few are chosen."

"Enough of these riddles," cried Judas, "I want to be let in on the plan, Jesus. I want to begin to prepare."

"Prepare by listening, Judas. Put on the wedding robe, my friend, not the battle armor."

Judas stomped off into the fields kicking at the ground before him in frustration. The rest of us began to wrestle with His words among ourselves. There was no clear understanding, but we knew Jesus would lead us where He wanted us to go, and for most of us, that was enough.

Later that evening, while the house was once again aglow with celebration, Rebekah, the storyteller, pulled me aside with a look of concern. She told me that bitter Leah had gone with a group of concerned Jews to the Pharisees to complain about the signs and the miracles that seemed to make no sense to them, and to warn them that Jesus was promoting some sort of Kingdom for the Jews.

She explained, "I have been told that the Pharisees are worried about the Romans hearing His Kingdom teachings as a threat to them, especially now with Passover approaching. The Pharisees fear rebellion. Caiaphas has even suggested they 'get rid of Jesus' to protect the rest of us."

I was shocked. Could they not see the Truth before them? Jesus was the Messiah, and this was our chance as a Jewish Nation to be great again. They ought to be embracing Him and following wherever

He lead. I still wondered if He planned on a battle with the Romans when He talked of the Kingdom, and I was now worried that we may not have the backing we would need. But Rebekah was not finished. She continued, "That is not all. Caiaphas and his chief priests also want to squash the belief they see growing. This means they must kill Lazarus as well."

"My brother? Why?"

"Well, his raising has brought many more followers to Jesus and they want to remove all signs of Jesus' power."

"I will warn them. They must be careful and I will talk with Peter. Maybe we can convince Jesus to go North again, away from Jerusalem until after Passover, let the priests cool down."

"Yes, but let us talk with them after the big feast planned tomorrow night. I will be here to help you and Martha serve the celebration. Let us have one more night of joy before we move to defend our Lord."

The next night, as Jesus was teaching before the party, some of the Pharisees came to listen in and one of them asked Him, "When, oh teacher, is this 'Kingdom of God' coming to our people?"

Jesus answered him boldly, "The Kingdom of God is not coming with things that can be observed; nor will they say, 'Look, here it is!' or 'There it is!' For, in fact, the Kingdom of God is among you."

He turned to those of us in His close circle and

said with His eyes intent on us to be sure we were listening, "The days are coming when you will long to see one of the days of the Son of Man, and you will not see it. They will say to you, ' Look there!' or 'Look here!' Do not go; do not set off in pursuit. For as the lightning flashes and lights up the sky from one side to the other, so will the Son of Man be in His day. But first He must endure much suffering and be rejected by this generation."

He turned back to the general assembly and continued, "Just as it was in the days of Noah, so too it will be in the days of the Son of Man. They were eating and drinking, and marrying and being given in marriage, until the day Noah entered the ark, and the flood came and destroyed all of them. Likewise, just as it was in the days of Lot: they were eating and drinking, buying and selling, planting and building, but on the day that Lot left Sodom, it rained fire and sulfur from heaven and destroyed all of them - it will be like that on the day that the Son of Man is revealed. On that day, anyone on the housetop who has belongings in the house must not come down to take them away; and likewise anyone in the field must not turn back. Remember Lot's wife. Those who try to make their life secure will lose it, but those who lose their life will keep it. I tell you, on that night there will be two in one bed; one will be taken and the other left. There will be two women grinding meal together; one will be taken and the other left."

With this, the crowd silenced and Jesus stepped down from His seat on the wall as to conclude the lesson for the day. Martha took His cue and addressed the crowd, "Tonight we celebrate the presence of our Lord with us. For tomorrow He must continue on His mission. Come, bring joy with you to our home."

The party was beautiful. Martha was in her true element as hostess, floating from guest to guest making sure each person had what he or she needed. As the musicians played and the mood lightened, I allowed myself to set aside my worry for a moment and drink in the beauty of my sister. I watched from the table: she glowed with radiance. There was not anger in her tonight over my clumsy attempts to help. This was her show and she enjoyed every moment of the work for which she seemed to have been made. She made every guest feel like part of the family and as if everything she could do for them brought her joy and brightened her smile.

When the time came for the celebrants to sit at the long tables for dinner, I prepared myself for the anointing I felt called to do. His teachings became increasingly difficult for us to understand and fear grew in my heart for my Lord. My concern had led me to prayer, and I was compelled to help prepare Jesus for the road ahead of Him. As guests settled, I brought forth the jar of nard perfume, broke it on the hard dirt floor of our front room and anointed His feet. Again, in remembrance of how I had anointed Him at my forgiveness, I wiped the perfume with my hair and prayed for Him as I knelt at his feet. I prayed that His Father would keep these feet on a safe path and would lead Him to where He was meant to be, which I now believed to be the head of a new Kingdom, the Kingdom of Heaven. He laid His hand on my shoulder and joined me in silent prayer, but we were interrupted by our money manager, as once again, Judas Iscariot bared his frustration.

Judas interjected his disapproval of me with the accusation, "Why was this perfume not sold for three hundred denarii and the money given to the poor?"

I sat back and looked at him, startled. He had never shown much concern for the poor or any of the needy people we had helped as we journeyed. In fact, many a time, Peter had to wrangle small coins from him to do the work Jesus asked us to do. The only time I had any conversation with him was when I had to obtain the money for accommodations, which were never cheap enough for him. So, I looked from Jesus to Judas, confused.

Jesus answered his accusation with an answer only a few of us, who knew of the threats, truly understood. He said to Judas, "Leave her be. She bought it so that she might keep it for the day of my burial. You always have the poor with you, but you do not always have me."

Again an allusion to His death. A heaviness pressed upon my heart and I began to understand that Jesus knew the dangers were real; He seemed to accept that death was closing in and I trembled with sorrow.

I looked to Peter, my confidant, and my concern was reflected in his own. I knew I would need to tell him of the warnings from Rebekah and together we would have to press upon our Lord to retreat to the north for the time being.

Chapter 16

I remember the week that changed everything...

When I approached them in the morning, I found Peter and Jesus already discussing plans. Peter pleaded with our Lord, "Jesus, I will go where you go, but is this the time to enter the city?"

"Peter, it is not for us to choose the time. It is the Father's time and we will go where He sends us," replied Jesus.

I took the opportunity to jump in, hoping the worries of a woman might sway the Teacher, "Lord, what good will it do the Kingdom, if we put our King in danger before it is here."

"The Kingdom is already at hand, Mary, and your King must fulfill the prophecies. My Rock and My Heart," he addressed us by His tender names for us, "You will not always have me, stay with me while I am here. This is the will of the Father. Do not so easily fall to fear. We enter the city today. Mary, walk with my mother who has just joined us this morning. Peter, you at my side."

With this we knew there was no convincing Jesus and so we obeyed. I set out to find Mary, His mother, and prepare for our procession toward Jerusalem. I was not surprised to hear she had made the journey for the festival, and I was glad I would get to visit with her. Secretly, I hoped to sway Mary to press her Son to head north for the time being, but when I found her, she was deep in prayer. So, I sat a ways away silently on the ground awaiting her and inadvertently hearing her private prayer.

"My God, I live to do your will. Give me the strength to be with our Son. From the day your angel appeared to me, I have offered my life to you. Behold your handmaid. See me on my knees before you and hear my plea. Is this what He was born to? Prepare me as I follow Him. I have not the strength but for You."

Sitting there observing Mary, I knew that I too had to follow her example and submit. My stubborn ways pushed against my spirit, wanting to control what I felt was spiraling out of control. There was chaos ahead, we all felt it, and as I closed my eyes in prayer I saw the dark clouds of a storm approaching. I wanted to stop the tempest. But this was not a storm to be quelled. So, I too fell to my knees and reaching toward the heaven asked not for my will, but for the fortitude to stand within His.

My fear did not subside, but a strength built up within me to hold me against the fear. As Mary finished her prayer, she walked to me as if she had known I was there and took my hand to help me to my feet. Together we rejoined the group who was busily preparing to head into Jerusalem for the day.

Before we left, Jesus called two of His closest twelve over and said to them, "Go into the village and immediately as you enter it, you will find tied there a colt that has never been ridden and a donkey; untie them and bring them. If anyone says to you, 'Why are you doing this?' just say this, 'The Lord needs them and He will send them back to you when He no longer needs them.'"

As they hurried off ahead of the group, many of our neighbors who had been with us celebrating Lazarus' return to life joined us in a procession toward Jerusalem. We walked in a slow steady pace, and before we had gotten very far out of Bethany, the two returned with the colt and the donkey. I could see them struggling from a distance, for it was clear the colt was not broken and that the donkey's stubborn nature ruled the creature. The sons of Jebedee may be called the Sons of Thunder, but their strength was tested today by these two seemingly mad beasts. We all stopped to watch hoping the animals might calm if the group ceased its procession toward them. Suddenly, the donkey bucked and thrust forward releasing the tautness of the rope in James' hand and throwing his captor to the ground. James sat up, bewildered and catching his breath.

"James the Great, huh? Seems my Father's beasts of burden are yet greater." We heard a laughter from the head of the group. It was Jesus. He had a laughter that started from the center of His being and echoed throughout His body as if it were gathering the whole spirit of the man before it burst from His mouth and infected every person within hearing range. At once we all fell to laughter along side of our teacher. It felt good to laugh. The situation had grown so tense of late that I forgot the joy we shared as a community. Soon enough James had recaptured the colt and dragged him toward his cackling audience.

"I am glad you all were entertained," James said as he brushed the dust from his cloak, "Jesus, you are mad if you think you will ride this beast. I'd gladly prepare him for supper rather than adorn him for a rider."

"Oh James, sometimes you must stand still and allow the storm to pass over you. You must not always pit your strength against it." As He said these words, Jesus calmly laid a hand on the neck of the agitated donkey and at once the beast relaxed and brayed, shaking its head as if to release the fight within him. As Jesus said these words about the storm, I knew he had been with me as I prayed earlier that day.

With the animals and their leaders calmed, the group draped their cloaks on the donkey for Jesus to ride and many of those who had joined the procession began to lay their cloaks on the ground. I went to the side of the road where I saw a man gathering palm branches to clear the edge of our dirt path. I picked one from his pile and played with it as we continued.

Walking up the road into Jerusalem I remembered the last big city we had all traveled to together. It was Caesarea. Jesus had brought us there for a short visit of teaching, but many of us had learned lessons from the city itself. Thomas, for one, had learned a painful lesson on the streets of vendors and conmen. There was a young boy, a gamester, who had three shells set upon a rock. The game he offered to play, for a bet of course, was for his opponent to choose which shell hid the silver coin of Caesar. If the person chose the correct shell, he won the coin. If not, he had to pay the wager. We had stopped to watch the boy outwit many a grown man before Thomas, with the confidence of a fool, stepped forward, "Let me win and tonight we shall all sleep on beds of feather in the best inn in the city."

We all looked to Jesus who just nodded and smiled. Thomas, growing more bold every moment, continued to persuade us of his ability. "Have no fear Lord, I will win. I have seen this boy's slight of hand and I know his tricks."

Again, Jesus just nodded and smiled with a look

of amusement. Thomas stared at the three shells as the boy spun them round and round mixing up their order and finally came to a sudden halt, the shells lined up perfectly. "Choose your fate, my friend," the boy said with the practiced voice of someone much older than his years.

Thomas boldly grabbed the middle shell and lifted it in triumph. However, beneath it was nothing but the polished stone it sat on. "What? How? I cannot believe it! I watched his every move!" Thomas gasped as Judas angrily brought forth the group's purse to pay the young gambler his due.

Jesus put his hand on Thomas' shoulder laughing, "My dear friend, I hope you learned you can not always believe what you see. In fact, soon you will learn that you must believe what you cannot see. Oh, and the coin is under the left shell."

"How did you see that?"

"I did not see. I know."

My mind returned to our present journey as Jerusalem grew in size before us. I began to sing quietly as I played with the palm I still held in my hand. Next to me, Mary joined in my song, which then spread out among the others. Suddenly, together in chorus, we felt bold and jubilant. After all, this was Passover week and before us stood the greatest Jewish City in the Land of our Lord. We were His chosen people and this was our festival to remember how God had saved us from captivity. It was time to celebrate. So we sang, "Hosanna!

Blessed is the One who comes in the name of the Lord! Blessed is the coming kingdom of our ancestor David! Hosanna in the highest heaven!" The words rose in unison above the crowd as Jesus proceeded to the gate as our King in Glory leading our triumphant parade.

Jesus raised his hand to silence us as we came within a stone's throw of the great gate and surprisingly it was a mournful voice in which He called out, "If you, even you", seemingly addressing the city herself, "had only recognized on this day the things that make for peace! But now they are hidden from your eyes. Indeed, the days will come upon you when your enemies will set up ramparts around you and surround you, and hem you in on every side. They will crush you to the ground, you and your children within you, and they will not leave within you one stone upon another; because you did not recognize the time of your visitation from God."

Hearing it as a battle cry of sorts, the crowd, which had now grown to a multitude, renewed our praise, waving palms gathered from the roadside and shouting from our hearts, "Hosanna! Blessed is the one who comes in the name of the Lord! Blessed is the coming kingdom of our ancestor David! Hosanna in the highest heaven!" We entered the city where many people came to welcome us, recognizing and calling out to the Great Rabbi, while others, who had not heard of the miracles and signs, questioned those around them about this odd royal procession.

Jesus led us all to the temple, dismounted at the base of the great stairs, and told the beasts to return to their home. Obediently as the winds are to His word, the donkey and colt turned and walked calmly through the crowd, exited the gate, and began to journey homeward. I watched the beasts trace their own tracks back toward their home as we climbed the stairs together. We entered the court surrounding the temple and discovered that the market where Jesus had found me selling doves so long ago was once again up and running. For a moment, I felt the old excitement as the throngs of people pressed against one another. The air itself intoxicated me with the thrill of the market.

I looked up and saw the sun reflecting off the helmets of the Roman guards who again stood watch from the porticoes that surrounded the vast Court of the Gentiles. They stood ready for any uprising that may happen during these large festivals. Was it fear or hatred that made them anticipate riots? I often wondered as I mused at their vision of us Jews boiling just under the surface. As the men I walked with stopped before the money changer's table, I saw a group of small children encircling a woman telling stories in the shade of the colonnades, and I remembered the stories Mary told us. I turned to her to remind her and found her gazing lovingly at the same scene. She grasped my hand and kissed it, smiling as we shared the memory for a moment.

However, we were interrupted by Jesus' commanding voice. He burst upon the crowd, "It is written, 'My house shall be a house of prayer'; but you have make it a den of thieves!" Again, a sadness came over Him as He looked around and saw that they had listened but for a short time to His teachings the last time He was here. I thought of the prodigal son who was led from his father's home by the distractions that this world offers. I blushed in memory that I too had been found soiling the good earth of the temple and silently thanked God that He had brought me here to see my old world from this new awareness. Many of the sellers scattered, but not all this time, and Jesus turned His back on them, and led us into the temple to pray.

Standing in prayer amidst the soft humming recitation around us, the only other sound I heard was the occasional clinking of coins dropping in the offering basket at the front of the enclosure. Many came to make offering, and it seemed the wealthy men threw their coins in to make an impact as the echoes of their money reverberated around the crowded court. Whenever a great clanging from the raining of an obviously large contribution fell into the basket, a soft murmur of approval paused the prayers for a moment and the giver looked about to be sure he would be recognized by all. Amidst these men seeking praise for their large contributions, Jesus noted an elderly widow approaching the front of the room.

He stopped rocking in prayer, touched my hand, and motioned for me to look up. I watched as she slowly made her way to the front with tired legs and shaking hands, leaning on a walking stick. Her shoulders folded in over her breast as if to shelter her withering body from the harsh looks of those around her, and we watched together in silence as He held my hand. A few haughty younger men almost knocked her over as she made her silent journey, and I felt Jesus take in a deep breath in unison with her as if He was helping to keep her balance.

At last she made it to the basket lying on the pavement and to me the crowd silenced and I clearly heard her two small coins drop from her leathered hands and ring against the growing pile of wealth. As the echo remained in the air, Jesus looked at me and said, "Truly, I tell you, this poor widow has put in more than all of them; for all of them have contributed out of their abundance, but she out of her poverty has put in all she had to live on."

As He finished, Thomas leaned over to us and remarked on how beautiful the temple workings were. The architecture and stonework were breathtaking and he and Andrew could hardly take their eyes off the carvings.

"They are truly a tribute to The Father," agreed Jesus, "However, the time will come when all of this is rubble and not one stone will stand upon another."

"When?" asked Andrew, leaning over his companion, "Will there be warnings so we may prepare?"

"Many will try and mislead you. Do not believe them when they say they know the end of time is coming. They will declare the time is here when wars erupt and famines break out. They will declare the time is here when earthquakes rock and epidemics kill. But, these things must come to pass and the end will not immediately follow. But many terrifying events will happen before all of this. You all will be persecuted for my sake. Many of you will be betrayed and killed. And everyone will hate you because of me. But have no fear! Not a hair on your head will perish. For if you stand strong, you will win your souls." Jesus placed His hand on Thomas as he shook, taking in the words of his Teacher, and then He continued, "Then, when the time has come there will be signs. There will be warnings, evil omens and portents in the skies, and on earth nations will be in turmoil, seas will erupt and roar. The people will fall to fear and their faith will be shaken. Then they shall see the Messiah coming on a cloud in glory. So, when you see these things, stand with courage for your salvation is near."

He paused and then, looking us squarely in the eyes He concluded, "I solemnly declare to you that when this all comes to pass the end of days is near. And though heaven and earth pass away, yet my words remain forever true."

We pensively left the temple, heavy with Jesus' words. And as we crossed through the emptying market we heard a voice in the crowd challenging Jesus, "Rabbi, we know you are an honest teacher and we know you will say the truth of God, even among dissenters. Tell us then, as you have broken up our market yet again and thrown the Roman money to the ground; is it right to pay taxes to the Roman government or not?"

Jesus stopped and turned toward the voice as we all did. He answered plainly, "Show me a coin."

The man, fishing in his pockets, found a coin and presented it to Jesus as he looked around to his friends.

"Whose face is on this coin? Whose name?"

"Why, the Roman Emperor's of course," the man said smugly, not seeing Jesus' point.

"Well then, give to Caesar what is Caesar's and give to God what is God's."

As He spoke, more came around Him, for His teaching was famous throughout the Jewish communities, and they came to hear Jesus: some out of curiosity, some of faith, some by chance stopping at this teacher among the many teachers this week in the temple courtyard.

As the evening drew to a close Jesus, along with His twelve, came back with us to Bethany. Mary, His mother, and I, along with Martha and Anna, sat by the fire and talked of the strange tension that was building in Jerusalem. The men seemed to feed on it without knowing it. Peter and James were becoming more bold in their defense of Jesus and we noticed several times that Judas, the strange quiet apostle, was not with the group while Jesus taught. Martha said she had seen him talking with a few of the Scribes in a shadowy part of the temple courtyard. Jesus' mother sat silent while we shared concerns staring into the fire with a quiet acceptance of all that was being said.

As we stood to retire to bed, she grasped our hands to form a circle and she offered up a prayer, "Father, I have given myself up to you. Let me have the strength to be with my son - your Son, on this journey He must make. Again I say to you, Here am I, the servant of the Lord; let it be done according to your Word."

"Amen" we responded, embraced one another, and retired.

Chapter 17

I remember our Passover Seder...

Over the next few days as Passover came to its climax, Jesus and I had few opportunities to walk by ourselves. Though He continued to teach every day in the temple and though His strength never wavered around His followers, I sensed privately He was troubled. On several nights I heard Him in deep prayer outside as the rest of us slept.

On the first day of Unleavened Bread, Jesus woke early and instructed Peter and John to take the lamb Ronen had provided to the temple for sacrifice. As I entered the group outside with Martha, Anna, and Suzanna, He called us over with His mother and sent us to town to prepare the place for the meal. He said to us, “Find a man who carries a jar of water and follow him to his house. Tell the owner that the Teacher sends you to prepare the Passover Seder.”

We nodded, each of us kissed Him and we headed into town. We found the man, just as Jesus had said we would and he led us to his master’s house. The wife of the home was happy to see the help, as she had begun the arduous task of searching out and disposing of any yeast in the household before the Seder. Such is the deep cleaning required each spring and there are never too many hands to make sure that the house is properly prepared. It was good to have a job to do; the uneasiness of the last few days could be worked out in the scrubbing of the house and preparation of the meal. Mary, who was like a mother to the whole group, worked in silence, but Anna talked incessantly about the festival crowds and the markets.

About mid-day, Peter and John appeared with the slaughtered lamb for us to prepare. As we began to skin the animal, Peter sat on the low wall and told us about the magnificent ritual only the men took part in each year. His usual enthusiasm added zeal to the story as he relayed, “We carried the lamb, well ok, John carried the lamb,” he corrected himself as he saw John’s eyebrow arch in question, “to the temple and there were hoards of men. The great courtyards could hardly hold all the faithful, and the smell of dying animals and hot, crowded men seeped from the entrances of the temple. Inside the inner court men burdened with heavy baaing lambs, were waiting before the great bronze gate to enter and offer their sacrifice. As we waited, we sang the Psalms, 'O give thanks to the Lord, for he is good; his steadfast love endures forever! Let Israel say, 'His steadfast love endures forever.' Let the house of Aaron say," he paused here and waved his hands for us to join him in singing, "His steadfast love endures forever."

We laughed with joy at the vision of the unity of Jewish men in song as he continued, silencing his choir, "Finally, it was our turn and we presented the lamb to the priest. As John held it out for me, I slashed its throat in one strong and mighty stroke." We smiled at his pride and Anna giggled until Suzanna elbowed her to be quiet. Peter did not seem to notice our smirks, for he was swept up in the story as he stood up and began to act it out, slashing through the air to show us the strength he used. "As the blood poured from the lamb, the priest caught it in a bowl which was then passed to the Altar. Joining with the blood of the lamb from each family it bathed the great Altar as the singing continued, 'His steadfast love endures forever'..."

John interrupted, "Peter, we weren't still singing the same Psalm hours later when we got through that awful stinking line." He obviously was not as impressed with his charge of the morning.

"In story-telling," mused Peter, "Accuracy of mere details can be sacrificed for the spirit of the story, my friend. You've got to leave the people with a clear picture of the event, the impression of it, not a minute by minute running of meaningless detail. Come, I am sure the Lord looks for our return. Ladies, we thank you and we will see you later this evening." He grabbed mother Mary's hand, kissed her palm, and bowed slightly as they left.

"That Peter," Mary smiled, "He is a good man and he is certainly the rock my Son has called him. Well, I think we are ready to present the lambskin. Isn't it marvelous how time flies with a good story."

I looked down and she was right, we had skinned, cleaned, and tanned the lambskin without even realizing our hard work. Mary led us into the sitting room of the family and we thanked the master of the house for his hospitality and laid the offering before him in gratitude. He nodded his approval and his wife got up to hug each of us, "We are privileged to have the Teacher here in our home. Anything you might need I will fetch for you."

We returned to preparing the upper room for the Passover Seder and recitation of the Haggadah for Jesus and the twelve apostles. The owner of the house set up a roasting pit outside and took care of raising the lamb over the pit to be cooked. Just as the preparations were ready, we saw our group coming through the streets for the celebration. I was still upstairs with Martha, who was going over each setting place once more to make sure they had everything they would need, when I heard the shout in the street. I went to the window and saw the crowd following them with Jesus reaching out to the people from between Peter and James' protective coverage of Him.

They came in and we led them up to the room that had been readied. "Thank you," Jesus said to us as He reclined at the honored left side of the arch-shaped table. The others hurried to get a seat close to Him and settled on the pillows waiting for the long meal to begin. Suzanna had already begun to pour the first cup of wine, the Wine of Sanctification, as Jesus raised His cup and with the men recited the Kiddush, proclaiming the holiness of Passover. I ran out, realizing that in my haste to welcome them, I had left the basin of water for the cleansing outside in the hall. I returned with it just as Jesus began to search for it to wash His hands.

However, rather than pass the water, as was tradition, Jesus got up, wrapped a towel around His waist and turned to James who sat beside Him. He knelt in front of the stunned apostle and washed his feet. The rest of us watched in silence, not sure what to say. Without explanation, Jesus continued from one to another until He came to Peter. Peter recoiled his dirty feet from the Lord and cried, "Lord, you should not be washing *our* feet?"

"You do not understand now, Peter, but you will soon understand what I do for you."

"You will never wash my feet," Peter continued in protest of this humbling of our Lord.

"If I do not, you will have no share with me."

Peter looked at Jesus, considering what He said

and with realization that he could not say "no" to Jesus whatever He asked, he relented, "Oh, well then, wash not only my feet, but my hands and my head, for I am with you Lord."

Jesus smiled at Peter's wanting to dive in as usual, but said to him, "You are clean, and but only need your feet washed. However, this is not true of everyone here."

I wondered of whom He spoke, suddenly conscious of my own sins, but as I watched Him move on to the next man, I remembered my duty and hurried back down to where Anna and Suzanna were preparing the food. I returned to the upper room with the matzoh as they finished washing, and I set the flat bread on the table before Jesus. He broke it in half and handed me the afikomen, or afterbread, to hide in a cloth until the appointed time at the end of the meal. I nodded as the men continued their celebration.

Downstairs we were frantic to keep up with the preparation as the many steps of the meal passed. Martha made it all run smoothly, however, and kept us each to a task.

When we thought enough time had passed for the main part of the meal, I brought the afikomen back up to the room and stayed in the corner to see where they were in the celebration. What I saw and heard surprised me; for while the events followed the traditional ceremony perfectly, Jesus seemed to add something new to each promise of God. As time came to share the afikomen which represents the Paschal Lamb of Passover, Jesus took the bread and broke it, handed it around and said, "This is my body, which will be given up for you."

The men took the bread and ate in silence. I could tell that there had been heavy discussion during the meal and every eye and every ear was on Jesus. It then came time for the fourth cup of wine, the Wine of the Covenant. I quietly approached the table and filled Jesus' cup. He took it from me and, looking to each man, he said, "This is my blood, the new and every lasting covenant. It will be shed for you and for all so that sins may be forgiven. Do this in memory of me."

I was struck with these words by a vision of the lamb sacrifice that Peter had described earlier that day. Yet in my mind, it was not the lamb who bled for our freedom from slavery as it had in Egypt but Jesus. His blood ran over the temple altar and splashed into the cup held by the high priests. In my vision, I saw the cup passed around and blood dripped from the side of the mouths of those drinking. The temple shook and I was awakened from my apparition as the tapestry that hung before the Holy of Holies split from top to bottom.

Shaken, I fell to my knees before Him and wept. He brushed my hair with his coarse hand assuring all of us, "I will not leave you orphaned; I am coming to you. In a little while the world will no longer see me, but you will see me because I live, you also will live."

It was hard to leave His side, but I knew I was needed downstairs, and so I returned to the women in the main room. I could share neither what I had heard nor my vision, for I did not have the words to give to either. So, in silence, I busied myself with cleaning the wine cups used earlier in the Seder. As I held the cups, my hands trembled. The red wine that poured from them seemed to me thick as blood, but I could not look away.

Suddenly, the door upstairs burst open behind me and Judas came running down. He looked angry and yet somehow afraid as he pushed open the door and rushed outside. I followed him and saw him lean on the stone wall of the house to catch his breath. Reaching out for his arm, I asked him, "Judas, are you all right?" but he turned to me with a cold stare and only uttered a growl as he disappeared down the street in the direction of the temple.

I returned to the women and Anna asked me, "What was that all about?"

"I don't know," I answered, looking to mother Mary for any explanation she might have.

Mary only kissed us both and handed us our towels to direct us back to work. However, I saw a worry in her that scared me. Mary was always the one to calm us, to bring us serenity, and to guide us back to her Son for answers; but tonight, she offered no comfort. There was a stress about her that she would not share and that she could not hide.

It was not long after Judas left that the men descended the stairs following Jesus. Jesus stepped into the kitchen where we women were just finishing up. He tenderly approached his mother and handing her his drinking cup whispered to her, "Mother, your husband Joseph made this for me and I have carried it during my long journey. Now, I ask that you take it and keep it, for my journey is coming to an end."

"No, Son, do not tell me that it is time. I am not ready." She pleaded into His loving eyes.

"Tonight I will stay in the garden and pray. Mother, pray for me while you rest with the women." He kissed her, grabbed my hand that lay on His mother's shoulder and kissed it. And then they left. We cleaned the house, thanked our hosts again, and headed back to Martha's home.

On the way, Mary turned to me and, as if I was in on some secret, said, "You have the box with you, no?"

"Box?" I questioned.

"Long ago Mary, when you were a child traveling through Nazareth, my husband, Joseph, he gave you a box. Do you have it?"

I thought about her words, I had not seen her husband since I was a child. And then I remembered the elderly carpenter and the box I had treasured so long. Of course I had it with me, I always did. It was in my bedroll with the only treasure I had every found for it, the shell from Caesarea.

"Yes, I have it!" I burst out as the memories fit together in my head forming the picture of what she needed it for. For I had always believed it was a bush carved into the box, but now, as I studied the wooden goblet she held in her hand, I realized it was the space for a cup, this cup.

Chapter 18

I remember the night...

As we neared Martha's home in the growing moonlight, Jesus' mother grew more and more troubled and when asked, she replied, "The time has come."

"What time?" asked Anna, but Martha and I only looked to one another in silence. We did not know what was coming, but we knew it was on its way.

Mary tenderly took Anna's hand and said, "Do you know the words of Isaiah?" As Anna nodded, Mary recited them, "Surely He has borne our infirmities and carried our sorrows; yet we accounted Him stricken, struck down by God, and afflicted.

But He was wounded for our transgressions, crushed for our iniquities; upon Him was the punishment that made us whole, and by His bruises we are healed. All we like sheep have gone astray; we have all turned to our own way, and the Lord has laid on Him the iniquity of us all."

Tears slowly crawled down our checks as we listened and held each other's hands. Anna looked confused and in her naivety continued her questioning, "But I don't understand. What is happening? Why are you all crying? And why do the men beat their chests as they walk with our Lord?"

Mary looked to Anna, "Sweet child, follow my Son. He is the Way and you will soon see His light."

Anna softened and allowed Mary to wrap her arms around her as we continued home. While I had wanted to go with the men to see what was happening, I was glad I was here with the women for the comfort we offered one another. Mary's own patience gave us the patience to wait until we were needed.

She led us home and told us to sleep as best we could. Silently, she and I went to my bedroll and I uncovered the box she had asked for on our sad journey back. I opened it and as she lay the cup inside I came to realize it had been carved from the box. The box was not made for the cup but from the cup, the two were one. Could it have been established so long ago that I carry this half of His set? I gave the completed wooden piece to Mary, but she pressed it back into my hand and said to me, "you are to bare this grail, this Holy Grail, my daughter."

I returned the treasure to its place beneath my blankets and laid down to rest as she had suggested. However, we all struggled to sleep. The night was heavy, the cold was deep, and I found it difficult to settle my spirit to find rest. I lay, silent, trying to sleep, but struggling with an urgency to run back to our Lord, to hold Him, to kiss Him once more. Finally, realizing that none of us were sleeping, Mary rose and gathered us around the fire. We sat, looking to her for comfort and for answers to our anxieties. Slowly, softly she began to speak, and what she filled our hearts with that night was the story of Jesus' birth.

"Joseph and I had just recently married and I was heavy with the Blessed Child. Back then we had census calls from Rome. I look around and see that many of you are too young to remember, but maybe you have heard of them. Any time the Romans wanted, they called us to reshuffle ourselves like cattle back to our birth places to be accounted for. What the reason was, I do not know nor do I care, all I know is that I was now married to Joseph and had to go with him to Bethlehem. Pregnant or not.

"Joseph was a simple carpenter, but he did have one beast of burden that could carry me most of the way. I walked while I could, but when my ankles swelled and my back cried out for relief, I was happy to share my load with the old ass that walked with us. By the time we arrived in the small village of Joseph's family, the streets were full as a market, even though it was night. Joseph sought out relatives and friends from long ago, but they had all welcomed others who had arrived earlier. There was no room for us for that night. I felt Joseph's worry, for my slow travel had caused us to arrive well into the darkness. Finally, after knocking on every door, an innkeeper whom Joseph had known as a child offered us his stable for the night. He promised to send a midwife in the morning to check on me and wrapped the leftovers from the evening meal for us to take to our retreat.

"I welcomed the soft hay after the long journey and allowed Joseph to unpack and set up as comfortable a room as he could. He laid out a blanket for me upon a large bed of dry hay and herded the animals to the farthest stall. Unfortunately, that did not free us from the stench."

She paused as we all giggled at her wrinkled nose and feigned gag as she recalled sharing a shelter with the beasts. It was just what we needed, to recall Jesus at happier times, and what happier time could we share than His birth.

She continued as we quieted, "I remember watching Joseph set up our things and holding my tongue as he worked to remember how I had laid out blankets and unpacked the food in the rooms we had stayed in the nights before. He knew I could not work this night and dutifully completed all my tasks. Even if they were not how I would have done them, I remained grateful for his attention to my discomfort and his attempt to care for me."

Again the room shifted with smiles at the vision of Joseph fumbling to complete the tasks of a woman. Soft hands create soft homes, and this old carpenter must have struggled to match Mary's tenderness.

She continued, "The stillness of the night or the fact that I had stopped moving, I don't know which it was, but something called forth the Child. I was struck with such a pain that I winced and called out to my husband 'Help me!' I was but a small child myself, and I suddenly realized that my body might not withstand a birth. I panicked. Joseph, whose years assured him that my cries were healthy, comforted me by saying 'Mary, my dear, all women cry out in pain. It is Eve's legacy, there is nothing to fear.'

"Needless to say, his confidence did nothing to set aside my anguish and I begged him to find me a midwife, a mother, any woman to help me. He ran toward the main house, but all was locked up for the night and no one would answer for fear of thieves. And so, he returned, alone. Realizing he was to deliver the babe himself, he paled as my water broke, soaking the hay, the blankets, and his cloak. Never has there been a worse midwife", we laughed along with her as she remembered the clumsiness of her husband. "He groped blindly under my coverings, afraid to look at my bleeding and splitting body when finally he cried out, 'I found Him. He is coming!' I began to push with all my strength and finally, somehow, we were able to bring our Lord into the world.

"It was near morning and Joseph left me as soon as dawn came to fetch the woman of the house. A plump older woman showed up carrying a bucket of water herself as Joseph's hands still shook. We cleaned the babe while my dear husband returned to the realm of men and refused to enter the room until all was cleansed. Once the baby was laid in a manger, swaddled and healthy, the attending woman turned her attention to me. Bandaging my bleeding body, she questioned, 'why, the baby opened its own passage, how did you remain intact and yet become a mother?'

"The only answer I could give was the truth, "The Father. He is God's child.' The helpful woman smiled as if I was delirious from my ordeal and left in silence, still wondering about the new life in her stable.

"Now, my sisters, as we sit in vigil with fear in our hearts, let us remember that if Jesus could survive the incapable hands of Joseph and myself, what have we to worry about Him tonight?"

We all felt reassured and swore to finally get some rest. Returning to our bedrolls, I turned to thank Mary for sharing her story with us, but found her prostrate and in prayer. And so I joined her, lying on the cold ground, my arms stretched out almost to where they would touch hers, and I prayed.

I did not have the words to say, but prayed in silence asking the Father to fill in my words for me. Mary, our example, was silent as well. I felt a connection with her, and somehow I felt we were praying also with another, Jesus. It was as if He were with us in prayer. The stillness of the night was unearthly, for I heard no breeze and felt no warmth or coolness, and in this condition we stayed for a long time. Finally, as Mary sat up, breaking our prayer, she whispered to me, "Why is this night different from all the others?"

Her answer came before her question was complete as the door burst open before us and a frantic James broke into the room, "They have seized Him!"

Chapter 19

I remember the trial...

At once the whole house leapt to their feet and followed James up the path illuminated by the full moon that marks the Passover. The moment we heard our destination, Caiaphas's Court, fear took hold. Yes, he was a high priest, but he had been one of the priests appointed by the Romans and, known for his deception, was generally not trusted by the Jewish people. The further shock of a midnight council was one more reason to be afraid. Why had they not called the counsel in the light of day? Why hide it under the cloak of darkness? What had Jesus been charged with?

We rushed to the courtyard of the high priest to

find our answers and were surprised to see only a faction of the council and a few high priests and scribes who stood by Caiaphas in all his dealings. This was not legal. Where were the rest of judges? My questions were not to be answered as we were too eager to find out how it all happened.

In the crowd, Mary saw Peter and we joined him as he told us of Jesus' betrayal, "You know Judas wanted a revolution, a war. However, Jesus continued to shut down that talk and speak of His Kingdom beyond this world. Judas had had enough, I guess. He left us last night at Seder, storming out as if he gave up on us, on Jesus. We did not see him again until he came with the guards to the garden where we planned on spending the night."

"How could he betray Him like that?"

"The Deceiver uses the beauty of silver to divert our attention away from the truth," Mary stated flatly. It seemed to be no surprise to her, but her silence became more profound as she listened to the rest.

"She is right. He sold our Lord for thirty pieces. Oh, my friends, it was chaos. There were guards and blinding torches suddenly surrounding us. We could not see their faces until one stepped out into our group. It was Judas. He embraced our Lord and kissed him. Jesus only looked at him and asked, 'Do you betray the Messiah with a kiss?' Judas said nothing, only stepped back so they could seize Him."

"Did you do nothing?" I cried out as if these few men could stand against the Temple Guard.

"I tried, Mary, I tried. I drew my sword and slashed at the man closest to me. Instantly, he grabbed his head and fell to the ground as I lifted my hand to take another strike. But Jesus stayed my sword saying, 'Put up your weapon. Shall I not drink from the cup of my Father?' and then He knelt by the wounded man and healed the guard. This man who arrested Jesus was healed before us and yet, he was not moved. He did not give up his duty, but once healed returned to the arm of Jesus and led Him away."

Jesus' mother looked to the ground, hanging on Peter's sleeve as if for strength, and then turned to James and me and whispered more to the air around her than to us, "It is His will. So be it."

As the crowd settled, we found a spot where we could see Jesus already beaten and chained like a criminal. I cried out as I saw His face, swollen and bloodied by the temple guards who had dragged Him in. His slave-like appearance shocked me and I wanted only to go to Him and hold Him, nurse Him back to health. But we could not get closer than we were, for Caiaphas was ready to begin.

The proceedings started with witness testimony I could not believe. For He had healed these people, taught them, loved them, and yet many were turning on Him. Caiaphas asked Jesus to reply to every claim, but Jesus only answered, "I have spoken openly in the world. I have always taught in synagogues and in the temple where all our people gather. I have said nothing in secret. Why do you ask me? Ask those who heard what I said to them; they know what I said."

In answer another witness stood up and declared, "I have heard him teach that we must eat of his flesh and drink of his blood!"

The crowd gasped and a few muttered, "How can this be?"

But I remembered that lesson. We had lost many from the group that day in Capernaum. It was a hard teaching. The crowds who had followed us came more for free bread than His teaching and they demanded more. They had said to Jesus demanding more miracles, "Moses gave them bread from heaven."

This is where our trouble began. For, like the witness said today in the trial of Caiaphas', Jesus had said that He was that Bread. He said, "I am the Living Bread that came down from heaven. Anyone who eats this Bread shall live forever; this Bread is my flesh given to redeem humanity."

And, like here at this inquisition, they too had asked, "How can He give us His flesh to eat?" In fact, many of us questioned the same. However, we received no clarification.

Instead, Jesus only repeated, "Unless you eat the flesh of the Messiah and drink His blood you cannot have eternal life within you."

As I recalled this day long ago in the north and I saw how His words were used as accusation on this day, I connected it to His words at the Seder the night before and to the vision that had plagued me of His blood staining the floor of the temple. I looked to Him, expecting now we would get a further explanation of these words, but He stood, bleeding on the temple floor nodding sadly at the accusers.

Next stood a woman I recognized from Bethany. It was the old woman at wash day who had criticized the promise of a kingdom and who told me there was no place for a woman in Jesus' movement: it was Leah. She stood with her husband, for a woman could not speak in court, but the claims, I knew, came from her. Leah had been one of the first to question whether it was wise to upset the tenuous relationship between us and our oppressors. I remembered her bitter speech as we washed clothes together in the stream so long ago. And here she stood by her husband as he gave testimony, saying, "This fellow said, 'I will destroy this temple that is made with hands, and in three days I will build another, not made with hands.'"

This was what Caiaphas was waiting for. He leapt from his seat and faced Jesus demanding, "I put you under oath before the living God. Tell us if you are the Messiah, the Son of God."

Jesus replied, "I am; and 'you will see the Son of Man seated at the right hand of the Father, and coming with the clouds of heaven'".

The small faction of council buzzed in their nervousness and Caiaphas tore his cloak declaring, "Blasphemy!"

With that, this mockery of a trial was over as the guards closed in on Jesus, beating Him with their clubs. I covered my face, and Peter began to back away into the crowd; but Mary stood watching every moment determined not to lose sight of her Son. Caiaphas declared before the council, "Blasphemy must be punished with crucifixion!"

The words rumbled like thunder in my ears and I almost missed catching His mother as she fell between James and me. We held her up and followed the crowd outside as it was announced that Jesus would be brought to the court of Pilate. The corrupt priest had to bring in his cohorts, the Romans, because it was against Jewish law to have a man put to death.

We followed the growing crowd outside, but did not really know where we were going. James tried to keep an eye on the guards who held Jesus, while I supported Mary, keeping her from being carried away in the pressing mob. As we hit the streets of the city and headed toward the Court of Pilate, we once again found Peter. I was hopeful he would give us strength and help us get to the court, but he was distressed and I remember thinking I had never seen him wear his age so heavily. He fell to Mary's feet, crying, "Mother, what kind of disciples are we? Judas betrays Jesus and now he hangs from a tree by his own doing. I, whom He calls His rock, crumble with fright and deny Him. The others run in fear and hide."

"He forgave you before you denied Him, Peter. You are weak, but it is His strength we must rely on, not our own." Mary comforted Peter as he kissed her and left us to run ahead to witness the next proceedings. Somewhere in us there was hope that we would find a fair judge in the Roman governor. For whatever else the Romans were, they were thorough in their courts, a great point of pride for them.

However, Pilate's house was much the same: we arrived as more gave false testimony, and witnesses twisted the Teacher's words. To make matters worse, Pilate found no interest in dealing with what he considered a Jewish matter. Not only did he see this as unimportant, but he was also aggravated by being awakened so early by a mob of Jews. He had not had much luck in winning the Jews over, and so, he seemed to dismiss us. This case was of little value to him with either the Romans or the Jews and it was proving to be a waste of his time. What did get his attention, however, was when the crowd called for crucifixion. He was stunned, "What has this man done to deserve death?"

"He claims to be the King of the Jews!" someone cried out from the crowd.

"Is this true? Are you the King of the Jews? Do you not hear the many accusations they make against you? These are your own people?"

Jesus refused to reply, only stating, "You say that I am."

As I watched I wondered at Pilate's hesitation. He was swift to come down on us to quiet any hint of uprising to show the Roman emperor that he had managed control over this region. The most recent show of his power came when a group had marched on his palace demanding that the graven images be removed from Jerusalem. He did not respect our laws nor our people. So why then was he seemingly reluctant to put Jesus to death? I was just questioning this when James, who had stepped away for a moment returned to tell me, "Mary, I have just been told that Pilate's wife has had a dream."

"A dream?" I asked.

"Yes, in the dream she was warned against her husband's condemnation of a Nazarene. He fears his wife's dream and wants none of this. We may have a chance."

My heart lifted for a moment as I thought back to what I had learned about the Romans and their dreams. Often when a woman's dream had foretold danger, it was heeded or disaster struck. I recalled the story of Julius Caesar, whose wife begged him to stay home from the senate the day he was murdered. Yes, this could work in our favor. Pilate would not want to ignore the dream of his wife. But as I looked to Mary, I saw only doom in her eyes. She knew what I learned later: this was in the hands of her Son not the governor of Rome, and He would not turn from His destiny.

As Caiaphas and his supporters chanted, "Crucifixion", Pilate searched for a way to quiet this growing trouble and, at the same time, to honor his wife's dream. I could see his face brighten as he thought he had figured a way out. He held up his hands for quiet and turned back to his palace. The shouts quieted to mumbles of curiosity with their audience gone and then turned to confused silence as he returned. He came forth with a prisoner, Barabbas, a murderer, led in like an animal by an impressively large guard. He offered the man to the crowd and called out, "In honor of your festival this week, I will release one Jew to you. Who would you have me release, Barabbas, a known killer, or Jesus, your king."

The mob, now in a state of fury, cried out, "Barabbas!"

Pilate stood stunned. He looked to an upper window where his wife watched the proceedings and shook his head at her. She lowered the veil that wrapped around her face and mouthed something to him. I did not know Greek, but I could tell he was affected by whatever she said. He tried again, but the crowd around us only grew more certain in their hatred of Jesus as Caiaphas led them in mad chanting.

James, Mary, and I clung to each other, praying for Jesus' release. His mother wept uncontrollably as each hope of victory was met with defeat by the enraged mob pressing closer to the Roman guard who kept them from ascending the stairs of Pilate's palace.

Finally, to calm them, it was Barabbas who was freed. Yet, still reluctant to kill Jesus, Pilate had Him taken to be scourged, hoping that would please the accusers. James and I followed Mary, knowing we had to stay by her side, but unaware of what we were about to witness.

Chapter 20

I remember the end...

Few were allowed to witness the flogging. The crowd did not have to witness the brutality that arose from their rage: only those of us who loved Him. We left the riotous roar of the courtyard and were led to a small patio near the prison. Stepping through the colonnades, I was frozen by the jeering circle of Roman guards hungry for the next criminal. My mind flashed to the rape I had endured under this same hunger for Jewish flesh, and I was overcome with the smell of manly sweat and the sound of their guttural grunts. I fainted.

When I awoke, James was holding me against an outer wall. He helped me to my feet and led me back to where Mary stood trembling at the edge of the punishment court. I followed her gaze to find Jesus bound in the middle of the Roman circle, chained to a post and stripped bare, making His flesh vulnerable to their every blow. Taking turns on Him, they released their fury as if personal hatred drove them to revenge. Strips of His flesh opened with each blow and I flinched at every stroke of the scourge. I brought my shaking hands to my eyes as His back seemed clothed in torn flesh and exposed muscle. Mary, however, stood with the strength of Maccabbees' mother, never turning her head from her Son, determined to experience every moment with Him.

He fell against the pillar as the guards chose another weapon: barbed whips that hooked into the muscle clearly striped across His body. Each time they struck Him, the guards had to step back and yank out the barbs that clung to the meat of His back. Every rip brought a grunt from the guard and a gasp from Jesus. I could bare no more and turned my head to James' chest to shield myself from His torture. Still, Mary stood unwavering. At last I thought He would die, the stone ground drinking all of His blood, when they stopped and carried Him away.

We were sent back to the courtyard now filled with a frenzied mob. I wondered if they had witnessed what they had sent Him to, would it have changed their hearts? Would they still condemn a man if they had to observe His condemnation? For them it seemed a party. They were awakened in the night by a high priest; the select few he trusted to do his work. And there was a common animalistic spirit growing among them like the swine herd in Gergesa. The people were intoxicated by evil: the glory, the fame, the approval of a man of power like Caiaphas, that is what they sought. Did they really hate my Lord? I do not know. I know many of them hoped to receive privileges, and I heard some of them talk of promises from the council as we made our way to the foot of the stairs.

When Jesus again was brought before us, His wounds were partially covered from the sight of the crowd by a mocking purple robe. It was one of Pilate's own, I believed, a show of royal power. Perhaps he thought the sight of Jesus' back and the torture he had received was too much even for those who had called for it. Upon His head, gripping His scalp was a thorn crown, further mocking His Kingdom as blood dripped over His eyes and turned his hair to red. Pilate turned to the crowd and said, "Are you satisfied?" pointing at the tortured and humiliated "king" before them.

With one roar, as if a single bloodthirsty animal, they cried out, "Crucify Him!"

I scanned the scene. Is this my people? I knew that it was not, not all of them. But even this small faction seemed unbelievable to me. Could God really be betrayed by any of His chosen? The crowd became violent as the hostility within them oozed and they continued pushing and shoving and shouting, "Crucify Him!"

They became a monster, with Caiaphas at the head directing the bestial lust for murder. Mary finally began to weep. She searched for mercy around her as we were being pressed upon by men who were not themselves, changed by their leader's hatred. She looked to heaven and begged for strength and I joined her in prayer.

The guards began to panic, looking to Pilate to end this riot before it began. And he did. Pilate, seeing no other way out, raised his hand to quiet the crowd, stepped to the bowl of water brought to him by a servant boy, washed his hands and said, "I will have no hand in this. You want Him crucified. Take Him".

His mother cried out, "No!"

James grabbed her arms to secure her from running to her Son. Mary was shuddering from head to foot and cold sweat dampened her hair. I feared a fever would come upon her and I looked into her eyes to check for clarity. Her soft steady eyes that I had so many times looked into for comfort now stared passed me as if I was but a ghost and she saw only the reality behind me. I could not get her to answer my prodding and together, with James, we carried her to the shade at the edge of the courtyard. As we fanned her with our cloaks, a servant woman of the house brought us a pail of water and a cloth to cool Mary's head.

"It is from the woman of the house", she said to me as I almost refused the help, believing we had no friends here.

With some cool water and a moment out of the growing heat of the day, Mary recovered her senses and again stood on her own with the staunch determination we had seen thus far. I held her hand to be sure I stayed with her as we followed the guards who led Jesus away. Leaving the courtyard, I turned back and looked up to the window of the palace where Pilate's wife was watching this tragedy unravel. Our eyes met for a moment and I felt her sorrow for us. In that moment we were not Roman and Jew; we were two women bonded by our mutual horror and by her generosity. "Thank you", I managed to mouth as she nodded, dropping the draperies to shut out the scene before her.

Out in the streets the crowd was very different. As we left the court and headed to the street where we knew we would find Jesus, we found our community again. Here, along the road, women wailed and touched our hands as we passed. Many offered Mary their love and sympathy with their eyes and men beat their chests as they heard the sentence of the Teacher they had come to love. We drank in their strength and with new resolve, searched for our Lord.

We found Jesus headed through town strapped to the beam of His crucifixion cross making His way through the sea of townspeople who always came to watch the criminals pass. Could this be the same King we heralded into Jerusalem not long ago? This procession of Our Lord, however was not met by palm branches to welcome a king, but a mix of tears from His supporters and spitting from His condemners tearing the crowd in two.

Neighbors, even families, stood together yet torn apart by their feelings for Jesus. A man throwing a rock at Him might stand next to his wife whose cries for mercy reached the heavens. Our beaten Lord broken already by the guards endured further malice by His own people now. They spit at his face, pushed the ends of the beam to make him falter, cursed His name, and spewed hateful cheers together as He struggled.

His mother, with James and me in tow, struggled to keep up with Jesus. Not wanting to break the lock of her gaze in case He could look to her for comfort, she pushed through the crowd and we followed. Thankfully, there continued to be, mingled within the hateful mob, those who helped us and made a path so that Mary could stay near Jesus the whole way.

As we left the marketplace and headed up a narrow street, He fell and was beaten. At this point, each blow met with bare nerve and muscle, which protruded from every visible area of His body. In anguish, Mary cried out to Him, "My Son!"

He managed to get to a knee, and showing the first sign of empathy I had ever seen in a Roman, one of the guards took His bloody arm and lifted Him to His feet. He began to walk once more. However, light-headed from blood loss, He fell again. This time the people parted and allowed Mary to run to Him. Tears choking her breath, she took her Son in her arms and said to Him, "Here I am."

Before He could respond, the guards grabbed her and threw her back into the mob, but He seemed to have reawakened and this time He lifted Himself back up and began again. The road was steep and rocky and the crowds pressed so close that many times He had to turn sideways to make room for the long beam strapped to His shoulders. By now, with beatings and continued injury, the white of bone appeared as He moved His body, forcing it to go on.

We reached the city walls and most who were there for mere sport drifted off back to the city. There were just a few from each side of the controversy who continued with us along the journey to death. The road out of the city toward the crucifixion mount was wider, but not nearly as worn, and without sandals His feet were now vulnerable to the heat of the sand and every scattered stone and pebble.

Suddenly, we saw Him stop a moment and tremble. His legs gave out and He fell a third time. Again, Mary could not get to Him, but strained against the guards. With Grace, Veronica, a follower, on the other side of the road saw our struggle to reach Him and broke through the front line of people to be at His side. She knelt on the ground and wiped the blood and sweat from His eyes with the hem of her dress so He could see. His dizzying vision searched out His mother, and Mary reached her hand toward her Son. Again, with her loving support, the man she still held as her baby in her heart, stood on His own, lifted the cross that would soon kill Him, and took a few more steps. His pace was slow and He now dragged one of His feet across the rocky dirt.

Our Roman accompaniment grew impatient and so they commissioned a man, who was just heading back toward town with the rest of the onlookers, to help Jesus with His burden. At first the man resisted, growing tired of this spectacle, but as he looked to the Man dragging across the ground, compassion drove him to help. Together with Jesus, he lifted the beam and they continued toward the mount. Finally, after a journey that would have taken a weaker man's life, Jesus neared the end; we were at the base of Golgotha.

Before the final ascension, I stopped a moment to catch my breath and scanned the horizon for something. I don't know what I looked for, perhaps it was more what I looked away from, for the scene before me grew too gruesome, and I was compelled to turn away from Jesus' pain for a moment. We were alone now: the few of us dear to Him, the guards, and Jesus. The last of the crowds had become bored since He had not reacted to their mockery and wondered back to the market or the temple, back to their daily routines. I thought of how we must already be forgotten in their minds as I watched them enter the city gate. Another criminal will pass in a few days with whom they will find sport and that man, too, will be forgotten. "Jesus is not one to be forgotten", I wanted to cry out after them, but they would not have heard me.

Our group had moved ahead of me, and I suddenly noticed how silent it was without the jeering and cursing that had filled my head for the last twelve hours. I craved separation from the truth of what was happening and so I stood alone for a moment. My gaze strayed out into the hills and I realized they were more silent that just the absence of the shouting. There were no birds, no breezes, no sounds. It was as if the Earth held its breath, as if the World was suspended, looking on our pitiful scene. I looked to the skies and found only the sun, bare and alone, scorching the ground in punishment for soaking up His blood. It was so intense that I was blinded for a moment as I turned back to the reality before me and could not find them on the path in front of me. I feared I had lost them as I struggled to regain my sight, but they were a slow moving band, and had not gone far, so that I hardly had to jog to catch up.

Reaching the peak of the Place of the Skull, Golgotha, the sun's heat was intensified as if it blazed directly on the plateau. We gathered as near as we were allowed and Mary and I wrapped ourselves in each other's arms. Behind us John, who had found us as the crowd dispersed, and James, our continued companion, stood holding us up. However, we were to lose the last of our strength.

All together we collapsed as Jesus gave into the exhaustion, hit the ground, awaiting His crucifixion. I was sure our hearts and His body could take no more when three Roman guards picked Him up and laid Him out across the tree carved for death. Stretching His right hand out, they had to bind it to the beam to keep it in place, for the damage to the nerve and muscle made it hard to keep it straight as Jesus' whole body seem to recoil into its center. Once the guards had His arm where they wanted it, they placed a large nail in the center of His palm. An angry, dirty Roman stepped forward raising a large hammer above his head. The muscles in the guard's arms shook at the weight of the tool and he grunted loudly as he allowed it to drop squarely on its target. Jesus cried out and His fingers collapsed toward the impaling nail as if to grasp at it. Was He trying to pull it out or to embrace the impending death? I could not know.

With the precision of a well-organized system, they moved to His left hand and again bound it to the cross. There were three of them who moved about Jesus as if simply completing a task. No expression framed the Roman's faces; I was not even sure they knew it was a human they worked on, securing Him to the wood. They looked as if they were in the middle of the mundane work of building a wall, nailing the pieces together for the latest temple commissioned by Caesar. In contrast, His mother felt every blow as mothers do. She grasped her chest as if to hold her heart inside her body.

The tears that fell onto her cheeks dried in the heat, leaving a mix of dirt and salt crusted across her face. And we could only hold her and join her cry to the Father.

Next, the efficient work crew rotated to his legs and two of them stretched them out together along the wood. As Mary shook in unison with her Son, the third guard pierced his feet clear through with an iron spike. Jesus could no longer scream in pain, only roll His eyes as if He would lose consciousness at any moment. I breathed in as the three men stood to discuss their next task. My own breath took me by surprise as I had evidently been holding my breath and I grew dizzy. I steadied myself and watched the guards, wondering what they were discussing. It was as though they were waiting for something before they lifted Him into place. Finally, a young boy, who had run out from the palace, burst into their circle and handed them a short board. It was His sentence.

"Yes! That's it!" cried one as he brought it over to where Jesus still lay on the ground pinned to his cross. He roughly unwrapped a bit of the twine that held our Lord's right arm to the beam and cut if off. Then, using it to secure the makeshift sign above His head where the Romans declared the crime of the condemned, the soldier stood back and called the other guards over. Together they returned to their work. The men began to tie long ropes to the crossbeams, and slowly they raised the cross into place. With a sudden shutter that echoed through the very ground we knelt on, it was jolted into place.

We stared in awe at what they had done to our Lord. I could not see the sign declaring His sentence and strained against the blinding light to see what they charged. John noticed me straining and read it aloud for us all, "Jesus of Nazareth, King of the Jews."

Alas, the mockery was not finished. Behind us came friends of Caiaphas who had been sent back up the hill to make sure the murder was complete and to report back the plan's success. One of the conspirators also read the sentence and complained, wanting the guards to add, "He claimed to be" to the sign "King of the Jews".

The Romans took little notice of the man and simply said to him, "What Pilate has written is written."

Defeated in their request, one of the priests returned to jeering at Jesus, calling out, "He saved others; let Him save Himself if He is the Messiah of God, His Chosen One!"

The guards joined the scorn, not yet satiated in their savagery, calling out to Him, "If you are the King of the Jews, save yourself!"

Even one of the condemned mocked Him saying, "Save yourself and save us!"

However, this man's comments did not go unchecked, for the other criminal rebuked him, "Do you not fear God? We indeed have been condemned justly, for we are getting what we deserve for our deeds, but this man has done nothing wrong." He turned to Jesus and pleaded, "Lord, remember me when You come into Your Kingdom."

Jesus replied to this faith-filled sinner, "Truly, I tell you, today you will be with me in Paradise."

His voice was strong and clear and had I closed my eyes I could have believed He was recovered. But I could not close my eyes and imagine this was a phantom haunting me in the night. It was daylight, no time for nightmares. We prayed, we cried, we beat our chests as the witnesses continued to taunt Him. The hours passed and finally, Nature began to react to the torture of Jesus. The lone sun, which had singed our faces, now turned from us as clouds covered the sky turning day to night. The winds picked up and pushed these last supporters of Caiaphas away with gusts of dust stirring up from the ground. John wrapped his cloak around Mary, Jesus' mother, and braced her as if she might be swept away by the storm. Together we waited.

For three hours more we waited by Jesus' side. The winds continued and the clouds gathered above us. Fearing the skies, the Romans moved away from the criminals, which allowed us free access. The Mother of Jesus saw her chance instantly as if she had been waiting for it and leaned on John to stand up. Without having to be directed, we joined her in the impending darkness with the wind tearing apart the world as our hearts tore at our very souls. John wrapped his cloak tighter around mother Mary and she welcomed his protection. As His mother reached up to caress His feet, Jesus looked down at us and uttered to Mary and John, "Woman, behold your son. Son, behold your mother."

John nodded in promise to look after Jesus' mother. We knew the end was near as His voice sounded dry and He gasped for breath between words. Wanting to comfort His Lord, James reached to the sponge drenched in wine and myrrh that was already lanced by a long spear and raised it to Jesus, but He turned from it and did not speak again.

We took turns touching His feet and saying our goodbyes. When I approached Him, I laid my open palm over the nail in His feet hoping the take the pain from Him. The coarse iron scratched my hands and His blood ran down my arms. I fell to the ground gathering His blood as if I could return it to His body, but my desperation was futile and James lifted me back to my feet so that I could look to Jesus one last time. I could not look up, but again went to His feet. I kissed them with my dry and cracked lips and stepped back allowing James to lead me to the ground since I was no longer steady on my feet. Mary then returned to Jesus and with a silent determination looked at her Son and beheld Him as best she could.

Suddenly the ground shook and the lightening rang through the air. Jesus looked to the blackened sky and cried with the last of His voice, "Father, into your hands I commend my spirit."

He died.

We stayed. Unable to leave, unable to move. We waited. For what, I do not know, but I stayed. Soon the guards came to break the legs of the criminals, a gruesome practice to hasten the impending death: a true sign of the impatience of the Romans. As they approached Jesus, one of them said that he had witnessed this man's last breath and that there was no need to break His legs. A third guard, tired of standing out in the wind snarled at them and turned to the body of Jesus hanging from the cross. He lunged forward and drove a spearhead into the side of Mary's Son, now an empty, shredded, and broken body. She gasped, unable to withstand any more.

As we huddled together we felt the shower from Jesus' wound and looked up expecting to see the last of His blood being drained. Instead, it was a gushing of water which poured out upon those of us left. It cleansed our encrusted tears and cooled our fevers of sorrow. Above us the wind silenced, and as if the spear had pierced the heavens themselves, rain poured down upon the earth. The guards backed up, shocked, and the man who held the spear threw it down as if it burned his hand. He gazed up at Jesus and uttered, "Truly, this was the Son of God".

With those words it became clear that it was from these guards that we were to request Jesus' body. Mary pointed John toward the guard who saw the truth at the end, and dutifully, John approached him for help in removing Jesus from the elements before the animals came seeking the carcasses. The guard spoke to the others who nodded as we waited for their answer. John returned to us and said that the Romans had agreed to give us the body. As the rain beat down upon us we again watched the mechanical work of the executioners.

Just as they had raised His cross together, they now lifted it from its hole and laid it on the muddy earth with His body hanging between the dead tree and the soaking ground. With heavy hammers dripping with God's own tears they reversed the crucifixion and sent the nails out of His hands and feet with swift blows. His corpse fell face first into a growing puddle of rain. Mary's body collapsed in my arms as limp as her Son's, and John and James rushed to pull our Lord from the mud and return Him to His mother's arms.

Kneeling in the sludge she held out her hands and they brought Him to her. They laid His body in her arms like a babe is given to its mother for the first time and she rocked with Him back and forth, caressing His face and brushing the bloodied hair from His eyes. We stepped back to allow her her mourning and with a voice larger than her petite and worn body she cried into the torrent of rain, "Our Son, Our Son! Look what they have done to Him!"

Chapter 21

I remember the beginning...

Because it was late in the afternoon and the Sabbath was drawing near, we could do no more than offer a quick burial with no formalities worthy of Him. At this point, even John and James abandoned us women, joining the rest of the disciples who had fled into hiding, fearful of further vengeance on the rest of the group. Only we women felt safe enough to see to this simple funeral.

The three executioners escorted us to the edge of the city with the body of Jesus. There we were met by several of the other women from our group who had been sent by James and John to help us in our sorrowful duty. We could not enter Jerusalem proper with a criminal's body, but had to await help from inside the walls. So, as we wondered what to do, I remembered one of our followers who might be able to help. I tentatively approached one of the guards, still not wanting to trust them even though they had helped us thus far. I asked the one who had cried out with us at Jesus' death, "Will you go to Joseph of Arimathea and tell him we await his help?"

He nodded and headed to the sympathetic council member's home. I hoped I had called for the right man, for I knew he was a believer in Jesus and that he was wealthy enough to purchase a tomb at this late hour of the week. When Joseph came to us, I found I had called the right man. He ran to Mary and kissed her, telling her he had awakened that morning to hear of the conspiracy and trial. He then relayed the rest of his story telling us that he had immediately gone to the temple to argue for Jesus' release.

However, by the time he arrived we had already moved on to Pilate's palace.

Once again, he tried to follow our progress, but being a step behind, had failed to catch up before the pronouncement of crucifixion. In desperation, Joseph had even tried to bribe Pilate, who seemed swayed except for his fear of the growing contempt at his door. Finally, with nothing else he could do, Joseph offered us the tomb he had recently procured just outside of town, feeling at least he could give us that with his wealth.

Even with a tomb ready, Sabbath law would not allow an entire ceremony, but only for us to place Jesus' body in the tomb covered with a linen shroud Joseph's wife had sent with him. There was no procession, no lamenting with the psalms, just a few of us women, Joseph of Arimathea, and the body of Jesus.

The tomb was not far from the city walls and by now we had stopped noticing the pouring rain upon our heads. It was a simple tomb, carved into the side of a small mount below the crucifixion hill. I caressed the chiseled rock walls as we stepped into what would be our Lord's home and I wept at their cold silent response to my warm hand. Again Mary took Jesus into her arms and rocked Him as if putting her Son to sleep on the linen stretched across the rock shelf awaiting its burden. Joseph waited until she had stepped away from the body before he folded the top half of the linen over the body in burial. We held hands, prayed, and wept. Unfortunately, even our solemn ceremony was cut short as Joseph noted the failing light outside and our need to return to the city.

With our sad business complete, we joined the other disciples in hiding. It was the beginning of the Sabbath, and so, we began with preparations. Peter, who still struggled with his own guilt, had assumed leadership out of duty even though his confidence was lacking. He sat in front of the group and directed Veronica, whom we had seen on the road to the crucifixion, to light the two candles. Beside me, Jesus' mother wept, clinging to her guardian John, and she tore her cloak in anger at her Son's death. We were a broken group, defeated and lost, with no direction, no teacher, no hope.

I did not break my fast with supper, but returned to my bed and lay staring blankly at the ceiling above me. It gave no answers and I wondered what we had been doing. What were we thinking? A kingdom for the Jews? A carpenter turned king? Had we been crazy? But Jesus, he was our Lord. As I lay there, I searched my heart expecting to find my faith in Jesus extinguished. And yet, I was surprised to feel belief warming the rhythms within me. I still believed Jesus to be the Messiah. Or that He *was* the Messiah, I corrected myself remembering His death.

Oh, I don't know what it was that I believed. If I listened only to my heart, "Jesus is the messiah" rang clearly, but logic reminded me of the gruesome scene I had witnessed. I had seen it, after all, and so I reminded myself out loud, "Jesus WAS the messiah". I guess the plan failed. But how could a plan of the Father's fail? As I lay grappling with the mysteries of this Lord, my mind slowly faded off to sleep and my dreams continued to confuse me. For hopeless as we were, my soul continued to cling to the everlasting gift of Hope.

I dreamt I saw Jesus, standing before me as the King of the Kingdom. Sitting beside the Father at the banquet table feasting in joy. We were all there, laughing and singing. Every sense of mine was tantalized by the dream: I smelled the sweetmeats and tasted the bitter wine; I heard the infectious laughter of Jesus and felt the warmth of His embrace. We were together. I slept on throughout the whole next day, missing Sabbath services, but remaining at this feast in my sleep. And when I awoke, early that Sunday morning, I sprang from bed as if I was going to meet Jesus. It was not until I entered the main room and saw the continued mourning of the barefoot disciples that I remembered the sorrow I had carried to bed. My heart dropped and I sought out His mother for comfort.

I found her sitting by the fire, staring into the dying flames, silent. As I touched her shoulder she looked to me and whispered, "We must go to anoint my Son. His burial must be completed."

I nodded and called for Joanna to leave her kitchen duties and join us. The three of us headed to the tomb to anoint Jesus' body with the sacred oils and spices. We were a silent funeral procession, not reciting the stages of life, but allowing our hearts to grieve in their own voices, inaudible to the world. I recalled the first time I had anointed His feet at the house of Simon. I wondered what had driven me there. Was I called to do this for Him? Had I sought opportunities to fulfill my mission unknowingly? The jar filled with the oils felt heavy today. I struggled to carry it, physically resisting my journey. If we didn't bury Him we could pretend that He was but away for a bit. I would not have to face the truth. I would not have to see my Lord dead. I shuddered at the thought of His pale flesh and empty eyes. I did not think I could do it and so I stopped in the road.

"Mary, we must," His mother said to me as if she new my hesitancy. Perhaps she too wished to stop and deny where we were going.

"I can not, Mother. I can't see Jesus dead. I cannot touch His cold hands and anoint His decaying body. I can't breathe in the air of His tomb. It will drive me mad. I can not." I wailed and fell to my knees begging her not to make me continue.

Joanna silently took me by the arm and raised me to my feet, "Mary of Magdala, you are dear to Him. There is no other who can help His mother in her task. Stand by Mother Mary, help her, be there with her."

I nodded, knowing she spoke with wisdom and love, and I reluctantly rejoined the mourning procession. Mother Mary took my hand, giving me strength while also leaning on me; together we were able to complete our long walk to the burial tombs.

This time as we neared the city walls to head to the caves of burial there were no spectators on the road to greet or to taunt us. We were ignored, as all the world seemed to have returned to their daily business. The city was still crowded with Passover celebrants, but the week was done and they were readying for their journeys home. I watched the bustling of packing and goodbyes without reaction.

They seemed to be in a different world or the three of us were in a different world: one intangible and separate.

Once outside the city the scraping of our sandals on the dry, rocky road was the only sound I heard. And the heat of the sun, that had been tamed by the city walls, was now free to burn down on us in the open. We walked, stopping occasionally to cry to the heavens or to help one another regain the strength for the next step. Finally, we neared the burial mounts.

As we approached the tomb, we noticed guards on either side of the opening. They were asleep in spots of shade still hidden from the morning sun, and so we approached quietly. A few steps further and we all stopped in shock: The great stone was pushed to the side of the entrance. The tomb was open, its door gaping like the mouth of a great beast waiting for its next meal. And the boulder taller than any of us and as wide as the three of us together lay disturbed, its impression still fresh in the ground before the cave.

"Who could have rolled this stone away without waking the guard?" Joanna questioned quietly.

"I do not know." I answered, picking up my stride toward the darkness.

Mary took our hands and led us past the sleeping guards. There on the rock hewn for His body lay the folded linens Joseph had used to wrap Jesus' body. But there was no body! Who would have taken Him? I grabbed Mary and Joanna's arms to hold myself up and found that they faltered as well. Together we managed to stay standing, but foolishly began to look around the tomb, as if the body could be misplaced in some corner. Mother Mary ran her hands along the walls, hoping the darkness hid her Son. But we could find nothing. Speechless, we faced each other.

Suddenly, we were joined by two men. Their tall shadows rose behind me as Mary and Joanna looked past me to the intruders. Defensively, I turned to face them, expecting the guards and instead was blinded by a white brilliance. I blinked in their direction, holding my hand up before me as my eyes adjusted to their light in the darkness of the cave. As their forms cleared before my eyes my mind recalled Martha's description of the man who beckoned her to my side the night of the rape. She had described him as carrying, " a lamp that set a glow about himself but not the room." Here was the same phenomenon and I could not understand what my senses and memories tried desperately to comprehend before me. The answer came to me from Mother Mary.

"Angels," she whispered, recognizing the celestial beings.

Together the three of us fell to our knees and adored them in their light. Mary smiled and looked to the one in front of her as if she knew him. He took her hand and brought her to her feet and they stepped away in conversation.

However, I began to weep, as the feeling of loss

of our Lord welled up inside of me. One the angels wiped a tear that rolled down my cheek and asked me, "Why do you weep?"

His question woke me to my senses and I was overwhelmed by his presence. He questioned us again, "Why are you looking in a tomb for He who lives? He is not here! He has come to life again!"

I scrambled to my feet and ran out to the waking sunlight. Running to find the body, for I could not absorb what the angel told me. No one followed me. Joanna remained on her knees, Mary with her companion.

At the entrance of the tomb I looked to the guards to assure myself I was not dreaming, that this was morning and the scene before me was truly happening. Jesus was gone. Angels spoke to me. I whirled around in confusion. Where do I go? Do I return to the cave? Do I return to hiding? As I searched the earth for some sign of direction, I saw another man.

My legs gave out and again I fell to the ground, gripping the rocks as if I would fall from the earth if I did not hang on. I could not speak. I could not move. I looked to this newcomer for any sign of reason to cling to. As my eyes adjusted, I concluded it was the gardener, for who else would be out here at this time? Oddly, he asked me the same question the angel had asked, "Woman, why are you weeping? Who are you looking for?"

I blabbered to him between what were now gasping sobs, "Sir, if you have carried Him away, tell me where you have laid Him, and I will take Him away."

I buried my face in my hands and held on to the ground as the spinning of the world suddenly made me sick. How could they do this? We have lost our Lord and now to desecrate His body by removing it from the tomb? How much more were we to endure?

Breaking into my thoughts, the man before me spoke again. However, it was not the voice of an unknown gardener as I had assumed, but the voice I knew in my soul, and my heart awakened as I heard Him call me by name, "Mary."

Chapter 22

His story continues...

"Master!" I cried out as I crawled along the dizzying ground knowing Jesus stood before me, but not understanding how. I reached for His foot wanting to touch my Lord, my Love, my God.

"Do not touch me, my heart, for I have not yet ascended to My Father." He cautioned me.

I started to rise to my knees so that I could look at Him, but His light shone brighter than any angel's and I squinted to distinguish His form. Slowly, just as the morning approaches in stages so that we can adjust, He came into view before me and I saw Jesus, alive. Gaining more strength, I sought out His eyes, and I found that as we looked into one another, the ground became firm once more and I was calmed. Jesus was alive and here He stood before me.

"Were you not killed? Did we not see you crucified? Did we not bury you?" I rambled as thoughts spilled from my heart directly out of my mouth.

"Yes, I died. And in three days I have risen. It is as I told you it would be. The Messiah had to be betrayed and handed over to evil men and crucified. I had to conquer death to deliver life."

Inside my mind battled with my heart. I wanted to know all the answers. Where had He been? What now? Could He rejoin our efforts? But my heart only wanted to be near Him. And since I was unable to give voice to any of my questions I simply sat at His feet.

He rested beside me, leaning on the boulder that had once locked His tomb, and together we watched the sun rising slowly across the sky in the peaceful silence we had often shared. We allowed ourselves to sit for a long time together. The morning passed as the shadows grew shorter across the earth at our feet and we communed in the stillness of the quiet new day.

I do not know how long it was before the other women, accompanied by the angels, stepped out of the tomb and joined us. His mother, her hands shaking and her joy-filled tears soaking her smock, approached Him as closely as He would allow. She too could find no words, only ecstasy in His presence.

With our group reformed, He spoke to us again. "Go. Tell my brothers to go before me to Galilee and I will meet them there. Tell them: I am the Way, the Truth, and the Life. He who believes in Me shall not die but have eternal life."

We were reluctant to leave Him, but deeming the urgency of the message, we obeyed. As we stepped out of the garden and onto the road again, Mary shouted with joy that as we now leave Him it is only to meet with Him again in Galilee. And so we ran, away from our Lord to again head toward our Lord.

Running like children at some great festival, we tossed aside the jars of ointments we had carried to anoint Jesus. We laughed as they crashed upon the stones that had punctured His bare feet as He carried the cross. We were exultant as we entered the shadows of the city walls and Joanna cried out to Jerusalem, "Your Messiah is come! Rejoice Israel!"

Mother Mary locked her arms in ours and we skipped into the city itself. We entered the gate as so many were leaving to return home after Passover that we had to turn sideways to fit the three of us together through the crowd. We would not unclasp our arms and so we played a game of twisting and turning, dancing through the unaware crowd until we reached the house where the men hid in fear.

"I have seen the Lord!" I bellowed as I opened the door to a mourning family in tears. They turned to me as the light of day broke their darkened room and gave light to their heavy moods.

"Bar the door woman!" admonished one of the men hiding in the shadows.

"I have seen the Lord! He is alive!" I repeated my message, "He said to me, 'tell my brothers to go to Galilee and I will meet them there.' He said to me, 'I am the Way, the Truth, and the Life.'"

Peter came forward and at first was gentle in his disbelief, "Mary, you are bewildered as we all are. But you could not have seen Him alive. We buried Him three days ago. It is the hysteria of women that sees ghosts and believes they speak with them."

"No, Peter. This was no ghost. Jesus is alive. Go to the tomb and seek Him if you like. He is not there."

"Mary," His fear-born anger grew, "You could not have seen the Lord. I will go and find out what happened."

"Are you to bother with the word of an hysterical woman, Peter?" Thomas mumbled from the corner of the room. "Why waste your time with fantasy. We need to discern our next move. Where are we to go?"

Peter silently considered what we were saying and, though he doubted my word, the Spirit opened his heart and he answered Thomas, "First, I will go to the tomb," and as he passed through the door he turned, smiled fondly at me and concluded, "and then we will go to Galilee."

Chapter 23

I remember my return to community life...

It has been many years since that time: the revelation of the Lords' resurrection and the day it was time to say farewell to my friends. Peter and the other apostles did venture north to meet with Jesus, and afterwards, they were sent all over the world to proclaim the Word.

I remained with my brother Lazarus, my sister Martha, and her husband Ronen, for my body was beginning to feel my age and my heart found comfort in our Bethany home. Peter wrote often and told me of triumphs and failures of spreading the story of Jesus and his vigor inspired me as it had when we were together. When he reached Rome his letters painted pictures of the great city and its inhabitants from every corner of the empire. He wrote of graven images larger than life adorning temples to so many gods he could not count them all.

Over the years, new members were consecrated to carry the Word and Peter wrote passionately of a man whose faith he admired though they were often on opposite sides of controversies about policies and doctrine. His name was Paul and he was actually a persecutor of our group; some still feared his infiltration was orchestrated by the Romans themselves, but Peter assured me Paul's conversion was true and that the Spirit was in him. Part of me continued to envy the dynamic mission of the apostles, but my heart was drawn to smaller audiences and a quieter life.

In Bethany and the southern region, Martha and I continued our teaching to the women with Lazarus by our side. With the women of Bethany, Martha and I spent our mornings at the well celebrating births, mourning with widows, and encouraging new wives. We continued our tradition of storytelling on washday and, while my skills did not improve, my joy in the home grew abundantly.

But that was to change too. For while I had envisioned a long content life at home, it was not too many years before we found ourselves moving again. I was not shy about telling of Jesus' resurrection and reminding the people of Bethany how

He had raised my brother from death. There was rebirth for all of us, I tried to teach the women at washday and the well as I had before. But the Pagans continued to migrate into the Roman Empire and their stories of demonics returning from the grave to wreak havoc on communities frightened my people. Soon, what was once celebration for the return of Lazarus became suspicion, and coupled with the resurrection of Jesus and tainted by the flamboyant stories of the demon "undead" from the pagan cultures in the area, fear developed into hatred.

One day as we awaited Ronen's return from the market, the elderly Rebekah darkened our door with news that Ronen had been attacked on his way out of town.

"They are coming for you," she gasped between labored breaths, "'Kill the undead', they cry. Oh, you must run! A mob of Pagans cursed Ronen's household and the powers that defy Hades here. As I speak, they gather in fear and by morning I am afraid they will come here, right into your house!"

She continued to relay the murder, trying to spare Martha the gore while maintaining her warning of their violence, "They came out of nowhere and yet every where: Pagans, Jews, our neighbors, foreigners, surrounded Ronen and they began to beat him and throw stones. All the while Ronen bravely declared his belief in the Risen Jesus. When at last his bones were broken and he could no longer fight against the stones, they dragged him back to the market, and hanged him before all who could see."

Without allowing time to mourn, Lazarus ordered we pack immediately and before the sun rose again, we had left our home for the last time.

We traveled east toward the sea and continued our teachings of Jesus as we visited small villages and stayed with camping nomads along the way. However, by the time we reached Caesarea, we were known and were met by Roman guards before the city gate. They handed us over to the Jewish authorities that could not risk another disturbance of the peace for fear their temple would be shut down.

"Well, well, if it is not more of the trouble I thought we had cleared out with that Rabbi Jesus," we recognized the voice immediately, it was Caiaphas.

Lazarus retorted, "Oh, you've been sent out of the temple and right into the heart of the Romans, huh Caiaphas?"

"Enough!" the scorned judge silenced the insinuation behind my brother's comment. "Again you are part of the problem, and it is only with my wisdom and leadership that we are allowed to worship here under Caesar at all. You all should thank me for getting rid of that 'King of the Jews'! Well, now you are in my den, and the lions here are vicious. We need no more hearing. I know the trouble you bring and therefore, at dawn you shall die."

"You can not condemn us to death," I screamed, "It is against our Law!"

"Oh, I have found a way, my sister, have no fear. You see, we are on the edge of the world here, the open sea laps upon our shore and there is no opposite ground for one to land upon. So, if I merely set you in a boat, with provisions of course, it is not on me if you, say, die at sea. I am only setting you away from us; death is perhaps the expected outcome, but I have no blood on my hands. I learned this 'bargaining with the divine' from my Roman friends, isn't it splendid!" and he laughed as our shock took our breath.

And so it was, as the sun rose the next day we were set upon the open sea without oars or sails and with little food and water. This way our death was assured, but our blood would stain no hand. A crowd looking for amusement in our fear chatted casually along the shore as we sat in the boat. With a cheer from his audience, Caiaphas announcing our sentence publicly, "Die upon the sea!"

"Kill them!" the spectators roared as their entertainment fed them the promise of blood: ours. It reminded me of the crowds at Jesus' death: some hated us, others just watched in curiosity as if our death was a sporting event put on by the Romans. Slowly our small boat stopped fighting the waves that tried to carry us back to shore and we began to drift out to sea. I watched as our homeland drifted away from us. Slowly it became just colors along the horizon until finally, there was nothing to see but open water and vast sky.

After we prayed together, Martha nervously began to tend to the rations as if we could stretch them out to last forever, while Lazarus tried to fashion oars from the seats in the boat. I fell prostrate on the deck and offered my soul to my Savior. I prayed for rescue, but at the same time I knew I was prepared to die for Him if that was His will. They stumbled over me and Martha snickered at what she saw as my "laziness" and my avoidance of work. But Lazarus trusted me and pulled Martha away, scolding her lack of faith and silencing her protest. And so we continued throughout the day.

As evening drew, my prayers unceasing, the waves settled and a quiet peace fell upon the vessel. Suddenly, Lazarus called out, "Man overboard!" Startled, I leapt to my feet and found him pointing out into the waters. Coming across the rippling ocean were three men of light: Angels! They approached us with arms open and smiles upon their faces. I recognized our celestial rescuers right away and thanked the Father for his deliverance. Saying nothing, they lifted our boat with us inside and carried us into the darkening sky. As we glided above the water, the three of us aboard drifted off to sleep as if the Angels had brought us rest as well.

We were safe.

Chapter 24

I remember Massilia...

When we awoke we were run up on a foreign shore. We were welcomed by a cool breeze rolling down from lush, green hills and the busy sounds of a bustling port. Above the hills stood tall cavernous mountains. We discovered that we were in Massilia, the largest port in the southern part of Gaul. What a welcoming community we found! And our stories no longer fell on deaf ears, but rose to glorify the Lord as we converted many to Christ Jesus' way. Our ministry continued with letters sent by our leaders, Peter and Paul, who encouraged steadfastness in faith and love of one another.

And again, I found a community of women in my life. A community of strength and beauty, of love and laughter, of hope and endurance. And they welcomed Martha and me in, taking care of us and sharing with us their stories as we shared ours. It was a close-knit village and we did our chores together as we had in Bethany. Here, as there, wash-day was the time of the week for sharing and fellowship, and of course, gossip.

I remember the week when word broke out that a young unmarried girl had become pregnant, and the talk of the river that day was of her impending stoning by the town. Many a righteous woman declared her death just; and I listened in silence to their verbal battery of this passionate young woman. Finally, one of the women hoped to bring me in to the discussion saying, "Mary, you are a virtuous woman. What is it that your Teacher, Jesus, said to do to these sinners? Does His law allow stoning of sinners as we do?"

I took a breath, asked for the Spirit to speak through me as I represented my Lord and I told them this story, "There was a young woman I recall who was about to be stoned for a similar sin as the law in our homeland is the same. The girl, I remember, had been married to an older man and was found to be carrying on with a young handsome boy nearer her own age. Adultery. Anyway, it was on our travels in a place filled groves of beautiful olive trees. In fact, it was on what is called the Mount of Olives that we found this scene.

"'Stone her!' a man demanded from the front of a growing crowd. At home it is the girl's husband who is given the power to determine her fate for such a crime. He lifted the stone and fingered the sharp edges without taking his eyes off the crumpled girl tossed out onto the ground before him. She lay on her side with her legs drawn up instinctively as if she were wanting to curl up into her self and disappear. The accusing husband readied to cast the first stone as was his right."

At this point the women who were listening to my story nodded, for their tradition of punishment was the same. I looked around and felt the heat of apprehension as they expected me to condone their violence. I again took a long breath and continued my story.

"The girl turned in shame as the rock flew from her husband's hand and ripped the flesh of her ear. Blood instantly came, feeding the crowd's frenzy and they vied for the next throw as their distain for her sin swelled in the summer heat. The girl closed her eyes and audibly prayed that the next blow knock her out, hurrying her death. The men of the town gathered their stones as the women freely began their own assault with words.

"'Slut'"

"'I knew her mother had not kept her close enough to home!'"

"'Poor man to find he has married a whore!'"

"They continued the onslaught of revenge as if everyone of them had been victimized by this girl's crime. The young bloodied face scanned the crowd through tresses of long brown hair for a kind face and her eyes rested on Jesus. Some of the Pharisees who were with the crowd caught this connection and approached Jesus saying, `Rabbi, this woman is an adulterer. The Law says to kill her. Do you agree?'

"Silently Jesus stepped into the center of the circle where the girl lay awaiting death and he bent down and wrote in the sand, 'I AM', the name of our God. He stood up and said to the crowd, "Yes, kill her, but only he who has not sinned may throw the first stone."

"The crowd murmured and the Pharisees became more insistent, "The Law says she must die. Do you question the Law?"

"Again in silence Jesus stooped and wrote in the sand next to 'I AM'. This time He wrote 'LOVE'.

I stopped my storytelling to allow the women around me to react. And they did.

"Your God, He is Love. Is that the message?" One of the younger women asked.

"Yes, and Love does not condemn us for our mistakes. You see, with Jesus' words, the crowd dispersed and Jesus forgave the woman and she repented. Love changed that woman's life where revenge and judgment would have ended it. If you are to be followers of Jesus, Love must rule your hearts."

We spoke little else that day and I was content to allow the Spirit to stir in them with this story of

Jesus. A week later, as we gathered for washday again, there was a new face among us. The young woman who labored under the weight of a growing baby was helped to the river by two of the older women and they sat her on a rock near the shore with her feet cooling in the water.

"Mary, this is Esmee. Her name means 'Loved one' in our language. Your story of Love saved her. We all went back and appealed to our husbands for her release to us. We told them the women of the town would take care of her and her child. They can deal with the boy as they wish, but we will care for her. She is one of us and we Love her."

I smiled and Jesus filled my heart with His love. I embraced Esmee and knelt to wash her feet. Such is a community of women.

For many years I found peace here in Massilia where I continued to teach of Jesus and to learn from the community and traditions of the people of Gaul.

Epilogue

At last, as age bore down on my tired body, my final call from the Lord came and I was beckoned into the wilderness of the steep white caves outside of the city.

Here the Spirit has brought me a peace in my hermitage to fill the last of my years: years I have spent in fasting, prayer, and rejoicing with the Angels. They tell me it won't be long before I am reunited with the Lord.

Just after my arrival to the caves above Massilia, Archangel Gabriel carried me to the loft just below the clouds and told me to watch the horizon. There I saw them coming. In shimmers at first like dropped confetti, but as they turned in the air together they became one string of satin ribbon caught up in the wind. The multitude of angels moved together as one wing in the air with a single purpose: the ripple of muscle rolling down the row of individuals carrying them closer. And at once I understood Christ's Church. We, like these celestial beings, are one: His arms, His legs, His Body, and the more complete our faith in the collectiveness, the more fluent our journey together.

Each day of my retreat Gabriel has come and carried me away to this loft where I watch the morning angels move together as one and hear the heavenly host praise the Lord. And each day, they nourish me with His Body and His Blood in the very chalice I carry from our last meal together. In rejoicing and praise they carry me to ecstasy and each evening they return me to my cave to live awaiting my full reunion with Christ Jesus, My Lord.

As for my beloved siblings, Martha remarried after we had been in Massilia a few years. She married a sailor and makes a happy home overlooking the sea. And Lazarus, well, he has found his place as well. He joins Martha's husband on his boat for each voyage; he is at last a fisherman.

Bibliography

Biblenet.com "The Life of Christ: A Timeline" Biblenet.com, 1996-2001. http://www.biblenet.net/library/study/timeline.html

Cohn, Haim, Justice, Supreme Court of Israel. The Trial and Death of Jesus. Konecky and Konecky. Old Saybrook, CT, 1963.

Connolly, Peter. Living in the Time of Jesus of Nazareth. Oxford University Press: Oxford, England, 1983.

Deen, Edith. All the Women of theBible. Castle Books. Edison, NJ, 1955.

Englebert, Omer. Lives of the Saints. Barnes and Noble, USA, 1994.

Fullard, Harold, M.Sc. Philip's New Scripture Atlas. George Philip and Son, Limited, London, England: 1958.

Gafni, Marc. The Mystery of Love. Atria Books, New York, New York: 2003.

Gallagher, Fr. Timothy, OMV. Lecture Notes on Ignatian Discernment. Lanteri Center for Ignatian Spirituality, Denver, CO, February 2005.

Haskins, Susan. Mary Magdalen, Myth and Metaphor. Riverhead Books. New York, New York, 1993.

Isbouts, Jean-Pierre. The Biblical World. National Geographic Society, Washington, D.C.: 2006.

Kollenkark, Barbara. Lecture Notes and Training on Centering Prayer. Holy Name Church, Steamboat Springs, CO, 1997-2000.

Meyer, Marvin. The Gospels of Mary: The Secret Tradition of Mary Magdalene the Companion of Jesus. Harper Collins Publishers. San Francisco, CA 2004.

Pope, Hugh. "St Mary Magdalen". The Catholic Encyclopedia, Volume IX. Robert

Appleton Company, 1910. Online copyright, 2003, K. Knight. www.newadvent.org/cathen/09761a.htm

Readers' Digest. Who's Who in the Bible. The Reader's Digest Association, Inc. Pleasantvillel, New York, 1994.

Saint Mary Magdalen, the Beautiful Penitent. Saint Benedict Center, 1997-2204, http://www.catholicism.org/about.html

Smith, Gordan "New Testament Maps" J.B. Phillps New Testament. Pernarth, Wales, UK. http://www.ccel.org/bible/phillips/JBPNT.htm

Spangler, Ann, General editor. Catholic Women's Devotional Bible. NRSV. Zondervan Publishing House, 1992.

That the World May Know Ministries. "Herod the Great". Holland, MI. 1995-2007,

http://www.followtherabbi.com/Brix?pageID=274
5.